SHADES OF RED

For my sister, the Auntie Lisa,
and for Shadow, the Anti-Delaney.

Eagle Glen Trilogy

Shades of Red

kc dyer

A BOARDWALK BOOK
A MEMBER OF THE DUNDURN GROUP
TORONTO

Editor: Barry Jowett
Copy-Editor: Andrea Pruss
Design: Jennifer Scott
Printer: Transcontinental

National Library of Canada Cataloguing in Publication Data

Dyer, K. C.
  Shades of red / kc dyer.

(Eagle Glen trilogy ; 3)
ISBN-13: 978-1-55002-545-3
ISBN-10: 1-55002-545-7

  1. Time travel--Juvenile fiction. 2. Children with disabilities--Juvenile fiction. 3. Inquisition--Spain--Juvenile fiction. 4. Great Britain--History--Henry VIII, 1509-1547--Juvenile fiction. I. Title. II. Series:Dyer, K. C. Eagle Glen trilogy ; 3.

PS8557.Y474S43 2005   jC813'.6   C2004-907319-2

1   2   3   4   5   09   08   07   06   05

Conseil des Arts du Canada   Canada Council for the Arts   Canada   ONTARIO ARTS COUNCIL CONSEIL DES ARTS DE L'ONTARIO

We acknowledge the support of the **Canada Council for the Arts** and the **Ontario Arts Council** for our publishing program. We also acknowledge the financial support of the **Government of Canada** through the **Book Publishing Industry Development Program** and **The Association for the Export of Canadian Books**, and the **Government of Ontario** through the **Ontario Book Publishers Tax Credit** program, and the **Ontario Media Development Corporation's Ontario Book Initiative**.

Care has been taken to trace the ownership of copyright material used in this book. The author and the publisher welcome any information enabling them to rectify any references or credit in subsequent editions.

J. Kirk Howard, President

Printed and bound in Canada.⊛
Printed on recycled paper.

www.dundurn.com

Dundurn Press	Gazelle Book Services Limited	Dundurn Press
8 Market Street, Suite 200	White Cross Mills	2250 Military Road
Toronto, Ontario, Canada	Hightown, Lancaster, England	Tonawanda, NY
M5E 1M6	LA1 4X5	U.S.A. 14150

ACKNOWLEDGEMENTS

I spend a lot of time alone in the dark with a glowing machine. A lot. And in spite of my secret fear of the result-ant unnatural relationship that appears to be developing with my computer, there are fortunately a number of other generous and wonderful people who have helped give life to this novel. My deepest thanks go out to Dundurn publisher Kirk Howard and to editors Barry Jowett and Andrea Pruss for their sharp eyes and the clear vision they brought to this story. Special appreciation goes to the writers who held my hand through the process: Pamela Patchet Hamilton, Kathy Chung, Trudy Cochrane, Deborah Anderson, Bernice Lever, Moira Thompson, and the members of the North Shore Writers' Association, Canadian Authors Association, and CWILL. Thanks also to the global village of writers who have lent their time and expertise as readers of this work as it progressed: Linda Gerber in Japan, Kate Coombs and Lauri Klobas in California, Pamela Capriotti Martin in South Carolina, Marsha Skrypuch in Ontario, and the members of the CompuServe Literary Forum in all their eclectic and far-flung glory. *Muitos agradecimentos* to Humberta Araújo for her invaluable help with Portuguese dialogue. Gracious and dignified thanks also to all my non-writer friends who put up with my daily eccentricities whilst never rolling their eyes in my presence. And final thanks, as always, go to Meaghan for her critical acumen and her help in naming this book and to Peter for his unflagging support and unconditional acceptance of a mother who does not quite fit into the category of normal.

For the readers of this series and for the teachers and librarians who direct these readers, I hasten to note that more information about the history behind the stories, including study guides and further arcana, can be found at my website: www.kcdyer.com.

A bleak birthday dawns as grief gnaws at the heart,
A loved one heads straight for the flames.
Ancient wrongs still afire with no peace in sight,
Back to school and yet nothing's the same.

A mentor is missing, an old face is new,
And all is not as it should be.
Classes run, pencils scratch, but still floating near,
Is the ghost of a lost enemy.

Secret under the stairs found by curious eyes;
A labyrinth leads through time's door.
The slip of a leash; empty hands reach to clasp,
And the past is the present once more.

Friends are scattered like seeds, need again to unite,
But all hope dwindles down to a spark.
A priest keeps his counsel, his history concealed;
A menorah brings light in the dark.

Inquisition has spread, and the ash in the air
Tastes of nothing but death on the tongue.
Fear burns in the fires of a black Lisbon night
And chimes as each death knell is rung.

A hasty return leaves questions unasked,
Answers, while sought for, not found.
A trip into a trip, an unwelcome friend,
A new kind of illness abounds.

A monarch, a maiden with snapping black eyes,
And a brother and sister not kin.
Religion reforms. An absolute reign.
A journal holds secrets within.

Not the words of a witch, but the dream of a queen,
Brings to light one clear truth from the past.
Like a kiss lightly blown or a hero's last smile,
Bids farewell to a father at last.

Traveller no more, once a boy anger-filled,
Now a monk through the fire redeemed.
Death of a consort, one more woman scorned
Clears the way for a ginger-haired queen.

Scarlet blood, rusted death, crimson cloak, rosy hope,
Twisted time spirals back and ahead.
And reflects in the eyes of a girl and a dog,
As they seek out still more Shades of Red.

CHAPTER ONE

The first grey light of dawn crept in through the bedroom window and rolled across a neatly ordered desk onto the rumpled bedclothes. Darrell, sitting awake in the bed, drew her left leg up to her chest and watched as the light rose in increments as fine and steady as the ticking of a clock. She lifted her arm and stared bleakly at the watch on her wrist.

7:17 a.m.

January sixth.

For just over seven hours she had been fourteen years old.

Under normal circumstances, this would have been cause for some celebration, but as Darrell flopped back down in her bed, she'd never felt less like celebrating. Clear evidence of just how far from normal circumstances had become.

Without turning her head she reached over to her bedside table and felt around until she found her latest notebook, given to her as school ended for the holidays. Given to her by one Professor Myrtle Tooth.

The morning light in the room was too dim to allow for reading, so Darrell flicked on her bedside lamp and flipped through the book. Only the first couple of pages had been filled, but the brevity of her notes didn't make for any easier reading.

I killed Conrad Kennedy.

Looking at the words, Darrell realized that though she no longer felt sleepy she was still incredibly tired. But it *was* her birthday, and every fourteen-year-old should be able to enjoy a birthday. Tomorrow she would be heading back to the place she thought of as her second home, Eagle Glen Alternative School. A place peopled with eccentric and extraordinary teachers and attended by her two best friends in the world. She should be happy, excited, filled with anticipation.

Instead, she found herself suffocating under an emotion she thought she'd put behind her forever.

Anger.

Darrell grabbed her pen.

I may have killed him, she wrote, *but I should NOT have been the one in charge of keeping him safe.*

The phone tucked beside her bedside lamp shrieked itself awake, and Darrell's notebook flew onto the floor as she jumped in shock. She ripped the receiver from its cradle.

"What?" she snapped.

"Hey, whatever happened to hello? The sun's up, so I thought you would be, too."

"I'm fourteen, Uncle Frank. Don't you know that teenagers like to sleep in?"

"Yeah, I know that. I like to sleep in myself when I don't have to pour concrete, but that's what I'm doing today, so no sleeping for me."

Darrell could hear the smile in his voice. Uncle Frank. Always ready to see the bright side. It drove her crazy.

"Happy birthday, baby. Can I still call you baby now that you're a year older?"

Darrell sighed. "Yeah, I guess so."

"You know I'm coming over to make you a special dinner tonight, right?"

"Yeah, I know."

"Well, girlie, you don't sound so thrilled about it, I hafta say."

"Oh, I'm thrilled, Uncle Frank."

"Baby girl, I can hear your eyes rolling right through the phone. Cheer up by dinnertime, okay? Are you blue because you're heading back to school tomorrow?"

Darrell shook her head. "No, I'm okay. See you tonight."

"Yeah, yeah. I can tell when you're feeding me a line, you know that? Anyway, I've got to go. Wet concrete waits for no man. *Veal parmigiana.*"

"What? Is this some new, trendy way to say goodbye?"

"No, goofy girl. I'm cooking veal tonight. It'll melt all your troubles away. *Ciao*, baby!"

Darrell looked at the receiver for a moment before replacing it on its cradle. Right. Eating politically incorrect baby cattle was going to solve her problems.

She dragged herself out of bed and leaned over to pick up the fallen notebook. She could close the cover on the words, but her anger and fear were not so easy to put away. Shivering, she started to get dressed.

This can't be happening.

The doorbell rang a second time, and Darrell's mother clattered down the stairs in high heels — evidence that the unbelievable *was* happening. When your mother is a doctor who spends all day on her feet, whose only concession to fashion is to trade her tattered Birkenstocks for Hush Puppies — when the day comes that a mother like that runs downstairs to answer the door wearing high heels, *stilettos* no less, it is but one more sign indicating the end of the world.

The end of the world as Darrell knew it, anyway.

Her birthday had started out bleak and somehow managed to get worse. Even a call from Kate hadn't helped. The last thing Darrell wanted to do was to set up a detailed plan for spring break when there was still snow on the ground.

"Thinking about spring is what you're supposed to do in winter," Kate had said. She'd also asked Darrell if she was mad at her mom and a bunch of other things besides, none of which Darrell had been in a mood to discuss. Kate, using her best be-cheerful-at-all-costs voice, had promised to meet Darrell at school the following day, and Darrell had only just remembered to thank her friend for the bouquet of balloons that gently bobbed in the hall.

Even a special delivery package of birthday brownies from Brodie hadn't helped.

Janice Connor slowed her trajectory by grabbing the scratched and worn newel post at the bottom of the stairs and peered into the darkened living room where Darrell was doing her best to hide from parental attention.

"What happened to the candles I lit?"

Darrell shrugged. She'd pinched them out at least fifteen minutes earlier. Trust her mother to have been too busy to notice.

"The one by the window was making the curtain smoke," she said, as innocently as she could manage. "I was worried they were a fire hazard."

The doorbell rang a third time, the chime taking on a frantic note.

"Coming!" called Darrell's mother in a bright, artificial voice, but she didn't make a move toward the door. Instead she smoothed her dress nervously and peered again into the living room. "You'd better just put the lights on then, kiddo," she said resignedly. "So much for ambience."

Darrell felt her temper flare. "Who cares about ambience, anyway?" she snapped. "You just don't want this guy to see the piles of your stuff behind the chair. If he's going to be your boyfriend, don't you think he ought to see how we really live?"

"Darrell! Women my age do not have boyfriends. But he *is* my friend, and I'd like him to be yours, too." Her mother's voice took on a wheedling tone as she shuffled a pile of books and papers farther into a dark corner. "Please just try to be nice, okay?"

Darrell rolled her eyes as her mother fluffed up her hair and scurried away. She was just leaning over to flick on the lamp when a blast of cold air swirled into the room. The cold condensed into a solid lump of ice somewhere just north of her stomach. She shivered.

The click of heels announced her mother's return.

"David, I'd like you to meet my daughter. Darrell, this is my friend Doctor David Asa."

Darrell could hardly bring herself to lift her head. Lethargy settled around her shoulders like a heavy shawl, and she fiddled with a piece of chalk pastel she'd found stuck under the lamp.

"Hi, Darrell." His voice, warm and deep, jarred her into looking up. Strange hearing a voice like that in this room — in this house that had been home to two females for so long. But when she did finally raise her head, Darrell was relieved to see that the man in front of her did not look at all familiar. His hair was blonde and stuck up from his forehead in a gawky way. In his hands was a small lumpy package. His glasses were completely fogged from the warmth of the room, so she couldn't see his eyes, but she could see enough of him to realize he was a stranger. And as far as she cared, he could stay that way.

"Darrell?" The frantic note in her mother's voice was back. "Can you say hello, please?"

"Hi." Darrell stood up suddenly and, avoiding her mother's eye, lunged for the stairs. "I just remembered some packing I have to do for school," she blurted and shot up the narrow staircase, taking the steps two at a time. "Nice to meet you," she called over her shoulder.

Her mother's embarrassed voice, stumbling through some sort of apology, faded into the distance as Darrell closed the door to her room and collapsed onto her bed. Her fully packed suitcase and backpack sat neatly by the door, ready to go. Desperate to take her mind off her mother's friend, Darrell pulled the notebook off the bed-side table and flipped open the cover.

It did the trick. Her eyes were drawn to the words neatly printed across the top of the page, and her stomach twisted with anguish.

How do you live with yourself when you've killed someone — even if that someone was your sworn enemy?

She closed the book, unable to bear the sight of her own written confession. This had been the worst Christmas holiday she'd ever had, and her mother's new boyfriend just capped it. Well — not actually the worst. That had been reserved for the Christmas three long years ago — the one spent still recuperating from the biggest loss of her life. Recuperating but never recovering.

Darrell lay back on her bed and willed herself not to remember the events of that time, but it was useless. Memories flooded through her, and she could taste bitter tears at the back of her throat. She rubbed her leg, tired from taking the steps so quickly, and rolled over to look out the low window. The elderly oak standing guard over her bedroom was bare of leaves now, the snow that had fallen on Boxing Day still clinging to its branches. Snow was uncommon in a Vancouver

December, but this year had been cold, and the snow had fallen and stayed and fallen again. A few traces remained, mostly in frozen lumps under bushes.

That year had been snowy, too. It had fallen on Christmas Day, but she hadn't seen it. The medication she had been given had done its job after doctors removed forever the troublesome joint that had once been her right ankle. But nothing could block out the pain of the loss of her father — and so she slept most of that Christmas, away from snow and presents and anything that brought the memory of his smile to her heart.

The front door slammed again, and another blast of cold air swirled up the stairs to announce the arrival of Uncle Frank. Darrell sat up on her bed and hurriedly yanked off her prosthesis. Sure enough, within minutes she could hear pounding feet on the stairs. Her door shot open and the cheerful, heavily moustached face of her uncle peered inside.

"Don't you ever knock? What if I'd been getting dressed?"

He chuckled. "Hey, the number of times I looked at your bare bum when I changed your diapers makes me think I wouldn't be seeing anything new."

Darrell raised her eyebrow skeptically. "Uh, I *am* fourteen, you know, Uncle Frank."

"I know. And I'm supposed to treat you like an adult now, right? All the more reason for you to be downstairs being nice to your mom's friend." He wagged an admonishing finger. "Your mom's really nervous about this, you know. She wants you to like this guy. So what are you doing up here?"

Darrell glanced away uneasily and touched her prosthesis. "It's — uh — it's only that my new leg is bugging me for some reason. I need to adjust it or something."

"Really?" Frank shot a sideways glance at his niece and reached down for the prosthesis. "Okay, let's have a look."

Darrell pointedly gazed out the window into the dark night as Frank examined the leg in his calloused hands. "Very cool machine you've got here, Darrell. What's this one do?"

She shrugged. "It's pretty much the same as my old one. Just bigger, because I've grown again, and this one is better for running. It's made of titanium so it's lighter and supposed to have really good cushioning. Still hurts a bit when I run up the stairs, though."

Frank sat down on the bed beside Darrell and gently placed the leg in her hands.

"I think you just need some time to get used to it. And maybe you gotta quit taking the stairs three at a time." He squeezed her shoulder. "Baby girl, I hate that you have to wear that thing with all my heart," he said softly. "But sometimes I think you forget how lucky you are to have so many people working to help you to walk and run and swim."

He stared at her for a long, quiet moment.

"And ski," Darrell added ruefully, at last. She rubbed a crease in her forehead and met her uncle's eyes. "I have a special leg for skiing, too."

Frank reached an arm around her. "That's my girl," he said. "I knew you couldn't stay mad at me for long."

He slipped a book onto Darrell's lap. "Look. I brought you something for your birthday."

Darrell took the book but didn't glance at it. "You know I'm not mad at you, Uncle Frank. I just can't believe Mom is bringing this guy over to our house. I mean, it's stupid to have a boyfriend when you're her age. And what does she need anyone else for, anyway? She's got me to keep her company."

Frank laughed. "Well, don't forget, this guy's got to pass muster with me, too. If I think he's a jerk, it's out the door on his butt, okay?" He got to his feet.

Darrell managed a little smile. "Okay."

"You need help to get that thing on?"

She shook her head. "No. I can manage. Thanks for the book, Uncle Frank. I'll be down in a minute."

As the door closed behind her uncle, the prosthesis shifted in her hand and knocked his book to the floor. Darrell slowly slipped on her new leg and tugged her jeans back into place before reaching down to pick up the paperback.

A hooded figure dominated the vermilion cover, one hand raised as if in plea or supplication. "W. Goldman," she read aloud. "*Escape from Spain.*" Ignoring the burning ache that settled into her leg as she stood up, Darrell clutched the book like a life raft and headed for the stairs.

Darrell lay disconsolately on the couch, fiddling with a piece of tinsel that had wrapped itself around her ankle earlier in the day. She was heading back to school this afternoon. Eagle Glen Alternative School. The best school she'd ever known — and the strangest. But all the things that made it special brought back terrible memories of her last days and the loss of Conrad. And life at home was no better.

Dinner last night had been a disaster. But when she'd dragged herself downstairs this morning, her mother had acted like nothing had happened. Darrell had ended up helping take down the tree, and the effort had sapped all her remaining energy. She collapsed on the couch, overcome by the lethargy that had dogged her the entire holiday season. Delaney dozed in a tight ball on the rug near the couch, snoring gently and making her feel sleepier than ever. Her new book sat on the table beside the couch, unread. It seemed too much like work to open the cover.

"Darrell!" Dr. Connor's disembodied voice floated down the stairs. "Time to get changed, okay? We've got to start for school in less than an hour."

School.

Darrell wrapped the tinsel around her finger and reached for the television remote. "I've set out my clothes, Mom!" she called. "I'll be up in a few minutes — just want to finish my show."

She flipped on the television. A news station showed footage of casualties in the latest skirmish in the Middle East. Darrell stared at the screen but couldn't determine where the mangled bodies were from. Were they rebels? Terrorists? Civilians? And how could anyone tell the difference? The flat snap of gunfire from somewhere behind the reporter onscreen startled Delaney awake, and he looked around blearily before settling down to sleep again.

Darrell gave up trying to figure out who was killing whom and changed channels. She stared at the flickering images through half-closed eyes. Scenes of war shifted into an arsenal of advertising. Ads for cars. Ads for diapers. Ads for beer. Darrell flicked through all the channels. Plenty of ads and not much else to see on Sunday morning television when a person's mother won't pay for cable.

The remote slid out of her hands as Darrell stared dully at the screen. The picture settled on a group of women in matching choral robes swaying stiffly from side to side.

"Probably an ad for some church," she muttered. Still, it saved her from thinking about her mother or school.

The music ended, and a man with a high blonde pompadour stepped onto the screen. He embraced each of the robed women in turn.

Darrell strained to reach the remote, but it lay on the floor just beyond her fingertips. The effort of stretching out her arm was too much, and she slumped deeper into the couch. The blonde man twirled to face the camera, his widely spaced eyes exuding sincerity. His voice flowed like hot caramel. "Do you believe?"

Darrell closed her eyes. This was almost enough to send her upstairs to get changed. Almost. But every time her thoughts turned to Eagle Glen, the same feeling of exhaustion descended, slowing her movements and dulling her thoughts.

"Do you *really* believe?"

Yeah, Darrell thought bitterly. *Yeah, I believe. I believe that everything I used to believe is wrong — that time and space are not what I thought they were and that bad things can happen to good people and that good things can happen to bad people and that it's all an exercise in the random behaviour of the universe.*

Her head hurt. She flung an arm over her eyes to block out the dull January light, and the muted voice from the television droned on, accompanied now by much cheering and applause.

"Rise up, people!"

Darrell pressed one ear tightly into the soft cushions of the couch, and the voice muted by half.

"You too can be saved!"

"*This* is what you wanted to watch? You can't be catching much of it with your head buried like that."

Darrell jumped and opened her eyes. "Uh — I guess my show is over," she said, glancing sheepishly at her mother's puzzled face. "I'll come upstairs now."

Darrell's mother reached over and placed a hand on her daughter's forehead. "Maybe you're fighting a germ, kiddo. You haven't been yourself for days." She slid into a spot beside Darrell on the couch. "David suggested last night that you might be disappointed that I had to cancel our Christmas trip to Italy."

Darrell shook her head. "No. I probably wouldn't have enjoyed it anyway. I'm not sick, I'm just a little tired. That's all." She fiddled with the tinsel. "I'm sorry about dinner last night, Mom."

Her mother sighed. "I shouldn't have brought David over for the first time on your birthday, so I'm sorry, too, kiddo. Anyway, you'd better get ready now. We have to leave by noon if I'm going to make the hospital on time." Darrell's mother ruffled her daughter's hair and walked over to the door.

Darrell glanced up to see her mother blush a little as she scooped a tiny menorah off the untidy top of the dining room table. "I've got to remember to thank David for this," she muttered and set it on top of an overflowing briefcase near the front door.

A menorah. What kind of a weird gift is a menorah? Darrell shrugged. David had presented it shyly to Darrell at dinner the night before. She had always believed that Chanukah was a kind of Jewish version of Christmas, but he had set her straight and told her the whole story of the festival of lights. Darrell snorted to herself. She could see through him. He was just trying to get on her good side to impress her mother.

Darrell scowled and leaned forward to grab the remote, when a voice from the television drove all thoughts of her mother's new friend out of her mind.

"What do you believe, crippled child?"

What? Darrell stood up and took a step towards the television. The screen held the face of the blonde preacher in full close-up, his black eyes blazing. His voice dropped to a whisper. "What do you believe?"

For a moment, time seemed to grind to a halt. *Crippled? Who uses a word like that these days?* Darrell's stomach clenched as she stared at the screen.

The camera panned out to encompass a tiny girl, blonde tresses rivalling those of the preacher's for brightness. She wore a frilly blue dress and white stockings over tiny, misshapen legs and supported herself on silver crutches. Darrell came back to herself and drew a ragged breath.

"I believe," the girl carolled.

"Then, walk, my child," commanded the preacher.

The little girl threw her crutches aside and, to the sounds of much applause and screaming, strode forward several steps and collapsed into the arms of the now weeping preacher.

Darrell snapped the button on the remote and the picture disappeared.

"I didn't know that shows like that were still on TV," came her mother's voice from the doorway.

"Neither did I," said Darrell, her mouth still strangely dry. "Piece of junk." She tossed the remote onto the couch.

"I used to watch those programs when I was a kid," remarked her mother as she hauled the laundry up the stairs. "I guess faith-healing never really goes out of style. And it got you off that couch, at least," she added over her shoulder.

Darrell paused with her hand on the scarred brown newel post at the base of the stairs. Adrenaline still surged through her. *I may not know what to believe, but*

I'm not crazy, she thought. *I knew that guy wasn't talking to me.* She grabbed the banister and took the old stairs two at a time, determined to give her heart a legitimate reason for racing in her chest.

Chapter Two

Darrell looped Delaney's leash around her wrist and joined a straggly line made up of a small group of students and a few travellers getting ready to board a commuter ferry. The line was short and moved quickly, as the ferry was small and serviced only the tiny water-side town of Sisters Bay and Eagle Glen School. Darrell caught sight of a familiar shock of red hair in the line and walked over.

"Hey, bed-head!"

Kate Clancy dropped her pack and let out her breath in a rush. "Sheesh! This thing is heavy!" She knelt to pat Delaney.

Darrell grinned, and her gloomy mood lifted a bit at the sight of her heavily laden friend. "Maybe if you left the laptop at home …"

Kate smiled back. "Yeah, that's likely. Why don't

you leave your foot home, while we're at it?"

Darrell pushed Kate into a seat on the ferry. "I'd do better without my prosthesis than you would without that machine," she said, not really kidding. "So what're you doing here?" She sat down in the seat next to Kate, and Delaney settled between their backpacks on the floor.

"My dad had to fly out on business this morning, so I'm stuck taking the long route. How about you?"

"Same." Darrell sighed. "My mom was called in to assist in a surgery at noon, so here I am."

"When does she leave for the big trip?"

"Tomorrow. I'll talk to her tonight, I guess, and then she's gone for five months."

Kate yanked her laptop out of its case. "Which brings me to our plans for spring break," she said, booting up. "I've made a list of stuff we should try to do —"

"Yeah. Whatever." The ferry rolled a little, and Darrell pulled her notebook out of her pack. She traced the letters of the first line, the paper like a sheet of ice under her fingertips. *I killed Conrad ...*

The words blurred, and she stared pointedly out the window at the waves, white crests slashing jagged lines between grey skies and black water. It was going to rain, and hard, any minute.

Kate looked up sharply. "Uh — is there a problem? Don't you want to come to my place for spring break?"

Darrell dragged her gaze from the turbulent ocean and sighed. "Yeah, it'll be fun. I've just got a few other things on my mind right now, okay?" The sick feelings about the loss of Conrad tightened her stomach into a knot, too painful to shape into words. She sidestepped into easier territory. "My mother has met some guy that she's working with in Doctors Without Borders and she's heading off to a war zone for five months. I've already lost one parent and now I just might lose another." She closed the notebook and twisted it in her hands.

Kate looked horrified. "You are *not* going to lose another parent, Darrell. Your mom will be away from any of the military action, won't she? She'll just be helping people in a hospital, right?"

Darrell tucked a strand of brown hair back into her ponytail and sighed again. The ferry nudged its way into the dock and she staggered a little as she stood up. "Yeah, she'll be working in a hospital. But which one? And how close to the fighting?" She thought of the bodies she had seen on the news that morning and shivered as she realized that the nameless dead had only yesterday been somebody's child. Or somebody's mother.

They followed the line of passengers off the ferry and then, as raindrops began to fall out of the sky, dashed onto a waiting shuttle bus. Kate flung her pack into an empty seat but clutched her computer case securely on her lap. A few other students trickled on to the bus before it lurched into motion.

"Your mom's wanted to do this for a long time, Darrell. Now that you're happy at Eagle Glen she can have a chance to give it a try," Kate said, keeping her voice low.

Darrell nodded. "I know. And I guess I haven't made life too easy for her over the past few years, so now that she thinks things are better for me —"

"She can do something for herself," finished Kate. "Now, let's get your mind off your worries and talk about school instead."

"Now there's a cheerful thought," said Darrell gloomily. She yanked Uncle Frank's novel out of her pack in order to tuck the notebook away.

"What are you reading?" asked Kate, looking relieved to change the subject.

"My uncle gave me this one," said Darrell, absently. "I haven't started it, but he usually gives me mysteries to read, so it'll probably be good."

"Great cover." Kate flipped it over and began to read aloud. "'A novel set during the fifteenth and sixteenth centuries, *Escape from Spain* traces the route that one Jewish family took to flee the horrors of the Inquisition.'" She shuddered. "I'm glad we never saw that part of the fifteenth century," she whispered. "The Renaissance was enough excitement for me."

Darrell shrugged and reached for the book. "I guess reading about it is all we'll be doing from now on."

Kate rolled her eyes and gave up. The bus turned into the long lane that led to Eagle Glen. Rain began to fall in earnest, sheeting against the bus windows and blurring the bleak view of bare-limbed cherry and maple trees that lined the drive.

Delaney put one paw up on the seat and pressed his nose to the window. "Almost there, boy," Darrell murmured, and his tail thumped in response.

The bus crested a small hill before circling a round in front of Eagle Glen. Darrell caught sight of the new nautical warning light standing sentinel on the coastline south of the school. From this angle there was no sign of any charred rubble — all that remained of the old lighthouse on the point. Less than a month ago she had watched as it had burned to the ground, its wooden frame lighting the night sky in a final, brilliant beacon. When the bus stopped in front of the school she stepped off, and the wind sliced through her jacket. Her mother might be heading to a war zone, but the glimpse of the warning light reminded Darrell that life had other ways of claiming casualties.

Kate ran into the school, trying to tuck her laptop case under her coat. Darrell and Delaney hurried behind through the downpour.

After shaking water out of hair and eyes, they hauled their packs and duffle bags up to the room they shared with Lily Kyushu. Kate called out greetings to other arriving students as she ran up the stairs, but Darrell dragged wearily behind her, eyes downcast. She collapsed in a heap on her comfortable old bed, but Kate grabbed her arm. "C'mon. I'm starving!"

"Go without me. I need to get some of my stuff organized."

But Kate was having none of it. As soon as Delaney curled up in his creaky wicker bed on the floor of their room she hauled Darrell back down the stairs and along the hall. Kate bypassed the student dining hall and beetled straight into the steamy school kitchen.

The air was redolent with tomatoes and herbs, and Darrell's mouth was watering by the time she sat beside Kate at the heavy butcher block table.

"Paella," said Mrs. Alma succinctly, bustling up to place a bowl of the hearty dish in front of her, thrusting a thick piece of peasant bread into her hand before Darrell had even finished saying hello. Kate beamed at the school cook and gestured wildly, her mouth too full to speak.

Darrell grinned a little too, her own appetite returning in the warmth of the kitchen and the cook's welcome. "Thanks, Mrs. Alma. This is obviously just what she needed."

To Ana Alma, the school cook, food was love. Judging from the way she practised her art, she adored the students of Eagle Glen. She stood still for a moment to ensure the girls had all they needed, then bustled off to continue preparations for the evening meal.

While Darrell ate she tried to let the atmosphere of Eagle Glen sink in and warm her heart the way the paella warmed her stomach. This was her third term at the school, and she longed to feel the sensation of pent-up excitement that had greeted her the previous terms. But this time, something was missing.

Or someone.

A dark head poked around the kitchen door. "Any food left for a starving traveller?"

Mrs. Alma bustled up to place a chair beside Darrell and Kate. "You'd better hurry, Mr. Brodie. Miss Kate is on her second bowl, and I think I may have to put on another entrée for dinner at this rate."

"Eating the school out of food again, eh Katie?"

Kate, mouth still full, made a face instead of attempting a reply. Darrell jumped up. "You can have my chair, Brodie. I've got a few things to do."

"Geez! Not even time to say hello?" Brodie gave her a mock frown.

"Hello," she said dryly. Darrell's spoon clanked in the sink as she deposited her dishes. She called a word of thanks over her shoulder to Mrs. Alma and waved at Kate and Brodie as they stared back at her quizzically. The paella had settled her nerves a little, and Darrell felt something akin to resolve as strode off down the hall towards the front office. It was time to face at least one of her demons.

Students were streaming in the front door of the school and luggage was piled everywhere. Darrell chewed on a thumbnail as she decided what to say to Professor Tooth. *It was my fault that Conrad got dragged back in time,* she thought stubbornly, *but if I am responsible for losing or even killing him — well, I'm fourteen years old. Professor Tooth is the school principal, she needs to share some of the blame. How could she let her students, her responsibilities, go traipsing around unprotected through time? Isn't it* her *job to keep Eagle Glen kids safe?*

The door to the office of the school was slightly ajar, and Darrell could just glimpse the silhouette of the school secretary behind her desk, the rise and fall of her voice resembling nothing so much as a chicken clucking as she talked on the telephone.

"You don't say! My goodness ..." Mrs. Follett waved Darrell inside, but as she turned back to her call, her voice dropped almost to a whisper. "Don't worry about a thing, Professor Tooth. Mr. Gill and I will keep everything under control until you return." Casting a wary eye at Darrell, Mrs. Follett slipped into the inner office and closed the door behind her.

Darrell's heart sank. Professor Tooth not here? She

leaned against the counter and strained to hear Mrs. Follett's voice; she was just considering creeping behind the counter to put her ear to the door when it reopened suddenly. Mrs. Follett emerged, her face looking pink and flustered.

"Can I help you, Darrell?"

"I'm not sure, Mrs. Follett. I'm here to talk with Professor Tooth, but from what I heard of your phone call —"

"Goodness gracious! Darrell, you're old enough to know it is terribly rude to eavesdrop on conversations. That was a private call."

"I wasn't trying to listen," said Darrell, relieved she hadn't had time to press her ear to the door. "I just heard you mention Professor Tooth's name."

"Yes. Well." Mrs. Follett looked more flustered than ever. "I'm sorry to say that Professor Tooth has been detained and will not be here for the first day back."

"Detained? Is everything all right, Mrs. Follett?"

"Yes, of course, dear. It's just that the professor is — has missed her flight back from Europe, and her return will be somewhat delayed."

Darrell turned to leave. "Okay, I'll drop by tomorrow to see her."

Mrs. Follett shuffled papers on the counter nervously, tried to collect them into a pile, and dropped half of the stack onto the floor.

"Let me help you with those." Darrell started around the corner.

"*No!*" screeched the secretary, bringing Darrell up short. "No, thank you, dear," she repeated more quietly, struggling to present an aura of calm. "I'll be just fine. And I'll let Professor Tooth know that you'd like to see her upon her return."

"Okay. Thanks." Darrell left the office as the school secretary dived behind the counter to pick up the stray papers.

"Upon her return?" Darrell muttered as she walked upstairs to the study hall. Her questions for the school principal would clearly have to wait. But what would keep Professor Tooth from attending the first day of the new term? A gust of cold wind blew through the front hall and slammed a door closed. She shivered. It was probably nothing. But a cold that could not be explained by the weather seemed to have settled into her heart.

Nothing. Apart from the teacher's name — a Professor Grampian — the course outline was completely blank. Darrell exchanged a glance with Kate, and they joined a group of students straggling down the hall to the old wing of the school. Kate and Brodie had been as surprised as Darrell was to hear of the absent principal, and the whole school buzzed with the news after orientation, presided over by Arthur Gill.

Mr. Gill was the art teacher at Eagle Glen but stood as second-in-command when Professor Tooth was away. His meeting had been informational and brief, and he had sent the first-year students off to find the new teacher, whom he explained would stand in for Professor Tooth in her absence.

"In her absence?" repeated Kate as they walked down the hall. "That sounds like she's going to be away for a while."

Darrell nodded. "My conversation with Mrs. Follett made me think it was just going to be for today, but now I'm not so sure," she said.

Lily Kyushu looked over her shoulder at them. "I just hope this new teacher isn't around long," she said, swinging her swim goggles on one finger. "The way you two are always going on about history with Professor Tooth, I thought I'd give it a try this term." She turned back to her friend Andrea. "I don't really like history, but Kate said Professor Tooth has a way of making the past really come to life." Kate winked at Darrell as Lily and Andrea hurried on ahead.

Darrell waited until the other girls were out of earshot. "That was really clever," she said disparagingly. "Now we're going to have Lily breathing down our necks in history class. What were you thinking?"

Kate shrugged. "It was just an idle comment — I can't even remember when I said it," she admitted. "Anyway, Lily and Andrea are so busy at the pool, they'll get their history strictly by the book."

"Yeah, well until Professor Tooth gets back, looks like we'll get our history that way, too."

"Is there any other way to get history than by the book?"

Darrell jumped at the sound of the quiet voice in her ear. She looked around to see a tall boy with a mop of vivid magenta hair who seemed to materialize out of thin air behind her.

"Paris!" Kate's face went almost as pink as the boy's hair and she started to babble. "We didn't see you. How've you been? Had a nice holiday? Geez, your hair looks great. I was just saying to Darrell —"

Paris grinned and cut her off. "Nice to see you too, Kate." He hiked his binder higher under his arm. "Funny, but you seem kind of nervous for some reason. Did I interrupt a private conversation?" He looked from Darrell to Kate as they struggled to find something to say. Darrell recovered first.

"Kate was just complaining about Professor Tooth being away," she said as smoothly as she could manage. "But I'm always ready for a new take on things, myself. We'll just have to wait and see, I guess."

Paris laughed out loud. "That's not what I heard, but I guess I'll just have to take your word for it, because here we are."

Eagle Glen had been built in stages, and before the turn of the twentieth century its first incarnation had been as a fishing lodge. Sometime during the First World War regal stone turrets had been added and it had been pressed into service as a convalescent home for injured and ill soldiers. After the wars the building had been used as a hospital and had even served as a hotel for a while, but it had only been converted into a school in recent years.

This hallway was in a seldom-used wing of the school. A cluster of first years including Lily and Andrea stood uncertainly outside the heavy wooden door.

Kate slipped through the group and pushed the door open, stopping just inside. The classroom was filled with the velvet darkness of a room that had been deserted awhile. Darrell followed Kate into the room and bumped her hip painfully on a table near the door.

"Ouch!" She slammed her books down onto the table and reached with both hands along the wall.

Kate slid her laptop onto the desk beside Darrell's pile of books and stumbled towards the only glimmer of light in the room, a thin line of yellow on the outside wall of the classroom.

"I can't find a light switch," complained Darrell as milling bodies began to fill the room, bumping and crashing into each other and various pieces of furniture.

"It's okay," called Kate over the muttering voices of the other students, "I think this is a ..."

The roller blind flew up with a clatter, flooding the room with rare winter sunshine and sending a cascade of dust down on Kate's head. Blinded as much by the light as by the previous dark, the students continued to bumble into one another until everyone finally found a seat.

Huge windows lined the outside wall of the classroom, and Kate opened the rest of the blinds before making her way over to where Darrell had pulled out a couple of chairs at a table near the front of the class. Kate shook the dust from her hair and coughed a little. "This place looks like it hasn't been used for a long time," she wheezed and turned to follow Darrell's puzzled gaze.

At the front of the classroom, a rumpled figure sat curled like a caterpillar in the teacher's chair, palms placed neatly on the desk on either side of a head adorned with hair as white and fuzzy as an old dandelion.

Darrell looked quizzically at Kate. "I've got a question," she said. "Who is that and what is he doing?"

"That's two questions," said Kate.

"I've got a more important question," came a voice behind them. Darrell looked around to see

Paris grinning at her. In spite of her disappointment with the missing principal, it was impossible not to grin back. Paris had a very catching sort of smile. "Is it still alive?"

Kate slid around one of the long heavy tables that apparently took the place of desks in the room and sidled up to the front. She stuck her nose right up to the face of the stranger and hazarded a guess. "Sir?" she whispered. "Excuse me — sir?"

A gentle snore was her only response.

Paris bounded up, delight oozing from every pore. "Not dead, I guess," he said, barely able to contain his glee. "Reminds me a bit of Lily for some reason." There was a haughty sniff from the back of the room.

Darrell grinned. "Leave Lily out of this, Paris."

Paris ignored her and spoke to Kate, who was still hissing in the apparition's ear. "I think you are underestimating the depth of the sleep involved here, Kate." He put his mouth right beside the ear that wasn't pressed into the desk. "Hello there," he bellowed.

Nothing.

The entire class looked on in silence, collective breath held, awaiting a response.

"Snnnnrrrrggghhhhh …"

"Not dead, but certainly unconscious," Paris noted, his eyes sparkling. "Perhaps — undead?"

"Nonsense, dear."

A shadow at the classroom door gathered itself into the person of Mrs. Follett, the school secretary. She bustled to the front of the room and smiled apologetically at the class. "I was a bit worried this might happen, so I thought I'd best pop down here and make sure Professor Grampian managed to get himself settled in."

Paris leaned over the table and whispered to Kate. "What a pair!"

Mrs. Follett reached down and shook the teacher briskly by the shoulders. "Professor Grampian," she trilled, her voice taking on a curiously piercing tone.

The effect was immediate. Professor Grampian lifted his fuzzy head from the desk top and looked inquiringly around the classroom. "Ah yes," he said, as though continuing a long conversation, "now as I was saying ..."

"Lovely to see you, Professor Grampian," warbled Mrs. Follett, aiming her voice directly into one of the professor's large ears. "Here is your first-year history class, all ready to go." She beamed at the group fondly. "Professor Grampian has kindly agreed to join us until Professor Tooth is able to return," she said brightly.

Darrell's heart fluttered a little, and everything that had been bothering her since her arrival at Eagle Glen seemed to fall into her stomach with a solid thump. Where was Professor Tooth?

Paris leaned forward. "This is going to be fun," he whispered, but Darrell was in no mood for jokes.

"Be good," she hissed, as Mrs. Follett began to address the class again.

"Now my dears, Professor Thaddeus Grampian has been an honoured teacher at schools all around the country for years, and we are delighted to have him. Please join me in welcoming him to Eagle Glen."

There was a polite spatter of applause, and Mrs. Follett blushed pinkly and scurried out of the room.

Professor Grampian cleared his throat and began to make his way around to the front of the teacher's desk. It was a painfully slow process, made even longer when the thought apparently struck him that he had forgotten something. He returned, a deeply thoughtful expression on his face, to his original spot behind the desk and retrieved the single sheet of slightly damp paper upon which his head had been resting. With agonizing slowness, he shuffled back to face the students.

In his chosen spot at last, Professor Grampian once again cleared his throat ponderously and, as though he were announcing the coronation, began to read off the class roll.

Taking attendance was done in every class at Eagle Glen, but as the groups were small and most of the students boarded at the school, it was a rare event for a teacher to call the names aloud. Done in a painstakingly slow manner in posh British tones, it was clearly more than Paris could bear. When Professor Grampian called "Mercer, P.," Paris poked Brodie hard in the back.

"Ow!" said Brodie, and glared over his shoulder at Paris. Professor Grampian nodded approvingly. Two names later, Professor Grampian called "Sun, B.," and Paris jumped to his feet.

"Present," he said with a grin. "And may I be the first to formally welcome you to our classroom, Professor Gramps."

"Thank you — er," the ancient professor consulted his notes, "Brady."

Darrell rolled her eyes. *Professor Tooth had better come back quickly,* she thought. *This place is falling to pieces without her.*

Darrell shivered. This old wing of the school seemed so much colder than the rest, and even after a week of classes, it felt like the temperature hadn't increased a single degree. Waiting an eternity while the new teacher lost himself in his own thoughts wasn't helping either. She drew an idle sketch in her notebook as he droned on. He seemed a nice enough old man, if a bit doddery. But this lesson — it was just like everything she loathed from her old school. Kings and queens, wars, dates. A pair of Spanish young people, he from Aragon, she from Castile, placed into an arranged marriage. Darrell felt dozy and had trouble following the professor's voice, reedy with age. She tuned him out entirely and concentrated on capturing the fuzzy aurora of hair that floated around his pink skull.

The bell to end the class finally rang, jerking Darrell back to reality.

"— and thus emerged one of the most evil persecutions in the history of the world, stemming from no less generous a source than one woman's love and belief in her God." Professor Grampian smiled genially at the class as chairs scraped and papers were rustled into piles. "Thank you all for your kind attention. We'll discuss the class project in more detail when next I have the pleasure of your company."

Darrell closed her sketchbook guiltily and stood up. "Class project?" she hissed as she watched Kate wrestle her laptop into its case. "What class project?"

Kate zipped up the case and joined the throng heading toward the dining hall. "You were in obviously in la-la land," she said dryly, and flicked the corner of Darrell's sketchbook. "Nice sketch of Gramps, though."

"Thanks."

"Yeah, well while you were off in space drawing pictures, the rest of us were forced to listen to the boring facts of the Spanish Inquisition."

"Boring is right." Darrell pulled her birthday novel out of her pack. "Maybe I'd better read this after all."

"It's got to be more interesting than Gramps's version," said Kate, stifling a yawn.

Darrell nodded. "I think I drifted when he started reeling off dates," she admitted.

"I hope this guy is only here for a couple more days," Brodie said from behind Kate. "In just a few lessons he's pretty much killed all the enjoyment Professor Tooth put back into learning history for me." He poked Kate in the arm. "Guess we need to talk about the field trip," he said.

Kate nodded.

"Well, which is it?" demanded Darrell. "A class project or a field trip?"

"The project *is* a field trip," clarified Kate. "We're supposed to form groups of two or three and organize a trip somewhere like the Museum of Anthropology."

"There's a whole archaeology section there — maybe we can make a side trip," said Brodie hopefully.

Kate rolled her eyes. "Kicking and screaming only, man. Like I'd want to spend any time at all staring at rocks after already dragging myself to look up a bunch more dates at some stupid museum."

Darrell stopped trying to stuff her sketchbook into her backpack and looked curiously at Brodie. "The Museum of Anthropology?" The inkling of an idea sparked like a firefly into her brain. She pulled Professor Tooth's notebook out of her pack and the sketchbook slipped right in its place.

"I have art class now," she said slowly, "but what if we meet in the study hall after school today and you guys can fill me in on everything I missed, okay?"

Darrell trudged into the art room, Professor Tooth's notebook clasped tightly in both hands. From the doorway she watched Brodie and Kate head down the stairs, Kate in the lead and Brodie running to catch up.

Chapter Three

"'Students have complete freedom to choose their own topic, within the constraint of the historical periods of the Spanish Inquisition or the Protestant Reformation,'" Kate read aloud.

"Okay, I do remember Gramps saying something about a lot of torture and mayhem," said Darrell, "so I'm pretty sure that must have been the Inquisition. But I have no idea what he means by the Protestant Reformation."

"Maybe they were reformatting their group somehow?" said Kate, scrutinizing the page in her hand.

"Uh — I don't think Reformation has anything to do with reformatting, Kate," laughed Brodie. "No computers before the twentieth century, you know."

"He said something about covering the Reformation later in the year," said Kate. "But he did give us that list, remember?"

The trio had pulled three overstuffed chairs together in the study hall and were reading over Professor Grampian's assignment by the light of the fire. The sun had long set, and only a few other chairs were occupied in the darkened room. Most first- and second-year students had elected to finish their assignments in the better-lit environs of the school library or dining hall.

Delaney was curled up beside Darrell's chair, snoozing with his head on the rust-coloured wool toque he had been carrying around all evening. Kate had closed her laptop, and Brodie fiddled with a new rock hammer that glinted in the firelight.

Darrell pulled out her notebook. "Yeah, here it is. 'The Ninety-Five Theses of Martin Luther.' I thought Martin Luther was a guy who fought for equal rights for African Americans."

Kate snorted. "That was Martin Luther King Junior. According to Gramps, *this* Martin Luther was actually a priest who got fed up with the way rich people in the Catholic Church could pay to get into heaven, so he made up a list of complaints and nailed them to a church door."

Darrell shrugged. "Pay to get into heaven? I guess I did miss some interesting stuff when I dozed off."

"That's okay," said Kate. "I got most of it down on my laptop. I'll run you off a copy of my notes."

Darrell nodded her thanks absently and pulled a broken piece of charcoal drawing pencil out of her pocket. "I was thinking about this class assignment," she said, twisting the pencil in her fingers. "When is a field trip not a field trip?"

"When it involves Eagle Glen Alternative School," answered Brodie with a grin. He pointed his tap hammer at Kate. "And I'm dying to find out just what Gramps has in mind. Every kid in the class has to partner up and put in a proposal. We have to raise the funds and plan the whole process. That much we all know. But where are we allowed to go?"

Darrell's voice was low. "I'm more interested in *when*," she said quietly.

"We're supposed to set it up to happen sometime around spring break," said Kate, reading the assignment sheet. "It says here that field trips can be taken in or out of school time, dependant on scheduling."

Brodie glanced at Darrell's face. "I don't think that's what she meant," he said.

Kate's head snapped up, and she instinctively peered around the back of her chair. "You can't be thinking about a field trip through *time*," she hissed incredulously. "Are you *crazy*?"

A burst of laughter came from Andrea and Lily, the last two students in the room. Kate turned on them furiously. "Will you keep it down? We're trying to get some work done here."

"Whatever you say, Kate Clancy," said Andrea mockingly.

"We've got swim practice, anyway." Lily scooped up her books. "See you later, *Darrell*," she said pointedly, and the two girls walked out the door. The sound of their laughter carried back from down the hall. Delaney rolled off the floor from his spot beneath Darrell's chair and, hat in his mouth, gently padded out the door behind them.

"Now she's mad at you," observed Darrell.

"I don't care," said Kate recklessly. "I wanted them out of here so I can find out what's going on in your head. Please tell me you don't want to take another trip through time."

Darrell leaned forward, still keeping her voice low in spite of the closed door. "I don't know what's going on in my head," she said. "I can't seem to sort it all out." She rubbed her right knee absently. "Maybe I'm crazy — but I can't forget about what I did to Conrad."

Kate ran her fingers through her hair in agitation. "What *you* did? Darrell, you didn't do anything to Conrad." She searched her friend's face.

"I left him behind." Darrell's voice was bitter. "I dragged him back through time with me and then he either burned to death in that fire or I left him stranded five hundred years in the past." She stood up abruptly and pushed aside the curtain that covered the heavy glass panes of the nearest window. "I killed Conrad Kennedy."

The night outside was dark and low clouds obscured the stars, but she could just make out the top of the new light standard, erected on farthest point of the beach south of the school. The light was shaded to the landward side, but the rhythmic flicker was reflected on the waves, cautioning night travellers to stay far from the rocky shore.

Brodie pushed his chair back and walked to the window, his hand lightly on her shoulder. "Darrell, Conrad made his own choices, you know that. He was running away from school. He was selling us all out — and besides, you didn't drag him with you. It was an accident that he was there in the first place."

Reluctantly, Darrell turned her eyes away from the spot where the old lighthouse had stood for so many years. The lethargy that had weighed on her throughout the holidays seemed to drag at her again, and she slumped back in the chair beside Kate. "You can say what you like, but I've been thinking about this for a while now. Somehow, Delaney and I are like keys in these doorways through time. Without us, nobody goes. You know it's true, Brodie; you tested it yourself. Conrad wouldn't have been there — couldn't have been — if I hadn't pulled him through time." She lifted her head with an effort and looked into his eyes. "And maybe I need to go find out what happened."

Kate grabbed Darrell by the sleeves and shook her. "Are you *crazy*?" she cried again. "We're not going into the past for our field trip! I want to go that museum in Vancouver, not back to the Renaissance to find Conrad."

In the firelight, Darrell could see Kate's face had gone the same shade as her hair.

"Besides," Kate blurted, "he might not even —"

"Still be alive?" finished Darrell. She laughed bitterly. "Well, I can guarantee you that he's *not* alive today." She pulled her legs up to her chest and rubbed her sore knee again. "I just have to figure out the location of another portal …"

"I can't believe this!" Kate looked beseechingly at Brodie. "Could you please talk some sense into this girl?"

Brodie opened his mouth to speak, but Kate jumped to her feet and started counting problems off on her fingers.

"One: you don't have a route into the past now that the glyphs in the cave are gone and the lighthouse has burned. Two: Conrad has been gone since before the winter break. That's more than a month ago. Whenever we've gone back in time, it's been compressed somehow, Darrell, you know that. Who knows where he is now? He could be anywhere. And three, even if we could find him, he'd most likely be dead. Professor Tooth is the only one who has any idea about what we've been up to and we're not even sure what she knows and what she doesn't. Besides, she's in Europe, and no one seems to want to tell us when she'll be back."

"Professor Tooth is a big part of my problem," said Darrell bitterly. "I need to talk to her and she's nowhere to be found."

"Darrell, you spent all last term trying to find a way to change the past," Brodie interjected. "Even with Leonardo's help, you weren't able to change things. You couldn't control the era you travelled to — the portals somehow just deposited you into a place in history. You couldn't go back and stop the accident that took your dad away. What makes you think you can do it now?"

"I just ..."

The door creaked a little, and they all jumped. A low shadow crept into the room.

"Delaney!" said Darrell. "Where have you been, boy?"

"He went out behind Lily," said Kate, stretching out her legs under the table. "He must've been just sniffing around outside."

The dog, the mass of wool still in his mouth, flopped back into his spot under Darrell's chair. She ran a hand down his soft golden back. "Still have that old thing? Where'd it come from, anyway?"

Brodie leaned forward in his chair and peered through the doorway. "Someone's coming. I think it's Paris."

"There you are you rotten thief." Paris closed the study hall door behind him. "Hand it over — I know you've got it." He bent down and plucked the object out from under Delaney's head.

Darrell looked apologetic. "Sorry, Paris. Did he steal something of yours?"

Paris waved the wad of rust-coloured wool and grinned. "This used to be my winter hat," he said. "I must've dropped it somewhere today, and I stopped to ask Lily and Andrea if they'd seen it. Lily said that she'd seen Delaney carrying something around in here, so I thought I'd check it out."

He held out what once may have been a rusty-red woollen toque. It now resembled a well-chewed dishrag.

Paris laughed and pulled the toque on. Large chunks of his freshly violet hair stuck out artistically through a number of holes. "This is the second time he's taken it this week. What can I say? The dog's got good taste in hats."

"Oh, Paris, I'm really sorry," said Darrell, rustling in her backpack for her wallet. "He doesn't usually steal things like that. I'll pay for a new one, okay?"

"Forget it — I like it this way." Paris posed like a run-way model and everyone laughed. "Besides, it'll give Lily and Andrea something new to talk about."

Kate raised her eyebrows. "Like they don't have enough to say already."

Paris nodded his agreement, and the exposed tufts of his hair bobbed gently through the holes in the hat. "That Lily sure can talk."

"You should hear her snore — puts her talking to shame," said Kate with a shrug.

Paris raised an eyebrow. "Try slipping on that little swimming nose-plug of hers while she sleeps," he suggested. "That might help a bit."

Kate's face lit up at the thought. "Not a bad idea," she muttered.

"So," he said, plopping down on a chair and putting his feet on the desk. "Anybody want a mint?" He popped a LifeSaver in his mouth. Everyone else at the table shook their heads.

"I have some of my own," said Darrell, patting her pocket. "Thanks anyway."

Paris looked around the group.

"An awkward silence," he said with a grin. "So what are we talking about, anyway?"

"Nothing. We're just leaving," said Kate hurriedly.

"Hmm," said Paris. "I could have sworn that a conversation of some sort had been taking place. But since you obviously haven't got anything better to do, I have something interesting to show you."

"Sorry, Paris, but I have some work to finish," said Brodie, shouldering his pack.

"You're the reason I came up here, Sun," said Paris. "This little discovery has some archaeological elements to it that I thought you might find interesting."

Brodie grinned and let his pack slide to the floor. "Okay, you've got me. What is it?"

Kate snapped her computer case closed. "Not me," she said shortly. "I need to talk my roommate here out of making a bad decision."

"That sounds interesting," said Paris, crossing one ankle over the other. "But does it compare to," he dropped his voice to a stage whisper, "a secret passage?"

Darrell sat up. "A what?"

"You heard me," said Paris, enjoying the result of his bombshell. He pulled his feet off the table and jumped up. "Interested?"

"Yes!" chorused Brodie and Darrell, nearly drowning out Kate's quiet "No."

"No?" said Paris, incredulously.

Kate refused to meet his eye. "Let's just say I'm a little anxious in enclosed spaces," she muttered.

He shrugged. "Fine by me. Are you two in?"

Darrell felt a sudden excitement course through her veins. "I'm in," she said quietly, and the hair on her arms tingled as though the room had suddenly filled with static.

"Me too," said Brodie.

Kate looked despairingly at Brodie. "Haven't you learned anything? I've tromped though enough caves and lighthouses with you to know that it's a little risky, especially with *certain people* for company."

Brodie shrugged. "We'll just go for a quick peek, Kate."

Paris looked baffled. "What are you talking about?" he asked Kate.

Darrell scowled at Kate. "Never mind," she said to Paris. "I'd really like to have a look. Kate can stay here with Delaney and then she won't have anything to worry about."

Paris looked from one face to another in increasing puzzlement, then shrugged.

"Well, whoever wants to come is fine with me, but I want to go now before the hall supervisor clues in to what we're doing."

"Who is on supervision this week?" asked Brodie.

Kate flipped open her binder. "Gramps," she said succinctly.

"Oh well — no worries there," said Paris. "Gramps spends most of his supervision time snoozing in the staff room." He jumped to his feet, pulled the toque off his head, and stuffed it in his back pocket. "Are you with me?" He pointed at Brodie and strode out the door.

"Be right back, Katie." Brodie grinned and hurried after Paris.

Darrell ruffled her dog's furry head. "Stay with Kate, Delaney," she said. "And no more stealing people's stuff." She glanced up at Kate. "I'll be right back," she added quietly. "I'm just going for a look."

Kate nodded with her hand on Delaney's collar. "Just hand me his leash, will you? I'll wait for you here." Her face was tight with anxiety. "Be careful anyway, okay, Darrell?"

Darrell pulled the leash out of her pack and tossed it to Kate. She dashed out the door in time to see Brodie heading down the stairs. She followed Paris and Brodie down to a door on the floor below the study hall.

"The library?" she puffed, catching up as Brodie flipped on the light switch.

Paris nodded. "I was in the music section at the back, and — well, I'll show you."

They were walking to the back of the library when the door burst open.

"All right! It *is* open!"

Darrell quailed inwardly. Not again! She turned to see Lily, still wrapped in her towel, though considerably soggier than before.

"I thought this place was closed for the night," she announced cheerfully. "But then I saw you guys all come in. This is great. I can sign out the books for my project now."

"The library is closed, Lily," said Darrell. "We just came in to look at a ..."

"... a poster," finished Paris smoothly. "For a music festival that's coming up."

"Oh," said Lily, looking damply disappointed. "So Ms. Rawiya isn't here?"

"Nope."

"All right. Guess I'll sign my books out tomorrow, then."

Darrell sighed with relief. "You do that, Lily. See you upstairs?"

"Okay." Lily started to leave and then hesitated. "Which music festival?"

"Uh — what?" Paris gulped.

"Which music festival? Maybe I'd like to go. Andrea likes folk — is it a folk festival?"

"No, not folk," said Paris quickly. "Uh — jazz."

Lily shook her head, sending droplets flying. "Ugh. Not a chance. See you later, Darrell." She wrapped her towel around her shoulders and bolted out the door.

"That was a close one," breathed Brodie.

Paris shrugged. "What's wrong with Lily knowing? She might think it's cool to see the secret passageway."

Darrell exchanged a glance with Brodie. "We've just found that a fast way to make sure everyone in the school knows something is to tell Lily a secret."

Brodie nodded. "And," he said quickly, "we don't really know anything about this hidden passage, right? How soon do you want the teachers to find out about it?"

"Not." Paris grinned. "I haven't exactly explored the place yet," he added. "When you see it, you'll understand. The main passageway drops down — it could go all around underneath the school, for all I know." He nudged Brodie. "Maybe we can even find a way to get out of Gramps's class."

"So what do you say we just keep it to ourselves for now?" asked Darrell, with another glance at Brodie.

Paris nodded. "Okay. It's just back here," he said, stepping though the stacks. "I was reading this book about Jimi Hendrix and I leaned right on this spot ..." He pushed against one side of the bookcase at the end of the row and the edge of the case suddenly popped forward. He turned around and grinned his triumph.

Brodie was beside him in an instant. He pulled the edge of the bookcase and it swung out like a door. "Simple catch and spring mechanism," he muttered, bending over for a closer look. "Seems a little rusty, though. I'll bet this thing is pretty old."

Darrell reached around the door and pulled one of the books out of the case. "Must be a strong hinge," she whispered. "Because these are all real books. This bookcase is heavy."

"Whoever built this didn't want it to just swing open by mistake," said Brodie, examining the clasp. "They've taken a lot of trouble to make sure it was carefully hidden." He looked closely at Paris. "Pretty amazing that you found it by accident."

Paris nodded. "I know. And all because of your dog, Darrell. Let's check it out." He pulled out a small flashlight from his pocket, flicked it on, and stepped through the opening.

Darrell grabbed Paris by the arm. "What do you mean, because of my dog?"

He stuck his head back through the opening. "I told you he stole my hat already this week, right? Well, I chased him in here and found him lying right at the back with his head on it. I grabbed my hat and saw this book about Hendrix and — well, the rest you know."

Her mind whirling with hats and dogs, Darrell let go of his arm. Paris slipped back into the dark doorway behind the bookcase.

"I'm right behind you." Brodie grabbed his own flashlight from his pack and followed Paris through the doorway.

"Just a second, you guys," said Darrell. "Paris, do you know how to open this door from the inside?"

Paris stuck his head back out through the opening. "Uh — no. I only went in a short distance the last time because I didn't have a flashlight."

Darrell stepped through the opening. "Then wait a minute. We don't want this thing to swing closed on us," she said and bent down to prop a hardcover book in the doorframe.

Paris started down the stairs, but Brodie put a hand on Darrell's arm. "Put your hand on my shoulder," he whispered. "Since you don't have a flashlight."

Darrell reached out her hand and followed Brodie into the passage. Within two or three feet a worn wooden stairway opened below them. Darrell and Brodie cautiously followed Paris's bobbing flash-light down the steps. The thin glow of light from above disappeared as the stairs reached a landing and changed direction.

Paris was waiting on the landing. "This is as far as I got before," he said in a low voice. Below the landing the surface of the steps changed abruptly from wood to rock and began a tight spiral down into the darkness.

"We must have worked our way under one of the stone towers," whispered Brodie.

Darrell felt a surge of excitement. "This passage might lead down to the cave, Brodie," she hissed in his ear. "Do you think Delaney led Paris here?"

"What was that?" asked Paris.

"I was just saying that it seems crazy to go on without more light," said Darrell loudly. "Why don't we come back tomorrow and bring some brighter flashlights with us?"

Paris bounded down the stairs. "Are you kidding?" he called back over his shoulder, voice echoing. "I want to see where this goes."

Brodie shrugged at Darrell. "Maybe you're right," he said in a low voice. "That dog is smarter than most humans I know. But we need to find out for sure. Besides," he said, holding the flashlight so that Darrell could see her way, "as long as Kate has Delaney, we'll be just fine."

Her excitement growing, Darrell followed Brodie down the tightly winding steps.

The air was dank and smelled of mould and mildew. The stone walls grew damp under Darrell's fingertips as they slowly worked their way downward. There was no handrail, so Darrell stepped carefully, all too aware of how quickly she would skid downward on the slippery stone steps if she lost her footing. For balance, she kept a hand on Brodie's shoulder as he descended in front of her.

"Thirty-nine," counted Brodie as they reached the bottom. His voice no longer echoed but sounded flat in the dank air.

As they shone their flashlights around at the bottom of the steps, several openings appeared before them in the wavering beams. To the right, rotten timber lay tumbled on the ground amid a pile of rocks. Only a small opening remained. To the left, timbers still shored up entrances to at least three other passages; Darrell knew more could easily lie outside the range of the flashlights.

"This is amazing," breathed Paris. "Why do you think all these tunnels are here?"

"Probably smugglers," said Brodie. "There was quite a bit of smuggling on this coast during Prohibition," he added.

"The building was originally a hunting lodge," said Darrell. "Maybe the hunters were supplementing their income by selling alcohol."

Paris shrugged. "Who knows," he began, when a long wail followed by a strange shuffling and bumping noise echoed down the stairwell behind them.

As they instinctively turned toward the noise, the beams from Paris and Brodie's flashlights converged on the bottom step.

"What — ?" began Paris, when into the light bounded a lithe golden form.

Kate followed, her face flushed. She stumbled down the last stair and tripped into Darrell's arms. "Bad boy!" she said breathlessly to Delaney.

The dog wagged his tail serenely, as if he had been out for a quiet stroll, and flopped down at Darrell's feet.

"What are you doing here?" said Brodie.

"How did you find us?" asked Darrell at the same time.

Kate shook her head in exasperation. "Your bad dog took off before I could get the leash on him," she said, frowning at Delaney. "He scratched on the library door — left a big claw-mark —" she added pointedly, "and pushed his way right in. I had to chase him down through the open bookcase at the back." She reached down and snapped his leash onto his collar. "Caught you, you criminal," she whispered, giving his head a pat.

She clutched the leash tightly and nodded at the pile of rubble and timber. "That looks like it leads to the cave in the rocks," she said, an edge of fear in her voice. She glanced at Darrell. "I'm not ready to go back there," she said. "And I don't think you should, either."

"What cave?" Paris looked interested.

Darrell reached out and took the leash from Kate's hand. "Nobody is going anywhere," she said. "We've seen everything we came down here to see."

"Not quite everything," said Paris, his voice echoing as he stepped through the entrance to a passageway. "I just want a quick look at this weird symbol on the wall …"

Kate shook her head. "Another time, okay, Paris?"

Delaney jumped up to follow Paris, and as he tugged Darrell forward she felt a familiar tingling in her fingertips. She whirled to see Brodie's puzzled expression and a mounting look of horror on Kate's face. Kate's fingers dug into Darrell's sleeve in a futile effort to pull her back out of the doorway. Darrell opened her mouth to yell, but her words of warning were ripped away by a massive surge of air that twisted and pulled her into oblivion.

Seconds later, Paris scrabbled on the dirt floor, the rocks and pebbles digging through his jeans into his knees. "What was that?" he gasped, and immediately regretted it. His mouth filled with what seemed like a century's worth of the dust that skittered and swirled through the old passages. His flashlight was gone, and darkness swallowed everything. His eyes felt glued shut with ancient grime.

After a minute or two he found he could breathe more easily, so he scrubbed at his eyes with a sleeve and felt around for his flashlight. No luck.

Now that the dust was settling, a strange silence seemed to descend along with it. Where was everybody?

"Darrell?"

No answer. He called the others, but even the dog wasn't making a sound.

"Brodie? Where are you guys? Kate! Delaney — here boy!"

Nothing.

Crawling along, he smashed his knee hard enough to make his eyes water and reached down in the dark to feel what he had hit. The familiar shape of the flashlight slipped into his hand, and he pushed the button hard. To his enormous relief, the light flicked on.

After a moment or two, he was able to orient himself. The weird wind that had whipped through the tunnel like a hurricane hadn't blown him as far as he'd thought — in fact, in front of him appeared the stone steps leading up to the school.

He staggered over to the staircase, wiping his eyes again on the sleeve of his shirt. The grit was incredible — his eyes were still caked with it. He sat on the bottom step and trained the beam of the flashlight up the stairs. Each step showed a thin film where the wind had stirred up the dust from the floor of the passages that stretched out before him. He felt completely disoriented, but got to his feet.

"I can't believe this," he muttered. "I've lost them somewhere, or that wind has sucked them down one of these hallways." He shone his light down the nearest passage, and his eye was caught by the outline the symbol he had noticed earlier, burnt or carved into the wooden frame at the entrance. He walked over and reached a hand out to touch the mark. Now that the dust had settled, it seemed as though the symbol bore the faintest tinge of red, and under his fingers the wall seemed to hold a strange warmth that vanished almost as he touched it. Almost.

His gut clenched and a strange nausea swept through him. Tiny beads of sweat sprang out along his hairline. "What's this all about?" he whispered. A glance behind him at the stairs showed no footprints. "They can't have gone up there."

The wooden doorframe under his fingertips had resumed its former chill, and Paris lifted his light to look again at the shape there. It was hard to make out, a charred black form against the weathered wood.

"Some kind of tree, maybe?" he muttered. He traced his fingers over the shape: eight straight branches emerging out of a single base. He shone his light at the wooden entrance to the passage on the left, the narrowest of the three. After a few moments of close examination he found a charred symbol there as well. "A lighthouse," he breathed. He placed a hand on both sides of the passage and took a deep breath.

"Brodie!" he bellowed. "Kate, Darrell, Brodie — where are you?"

Nothing.

He shone the light up the steps a final time and then turned and resolutely headed down the passage marked with the charred lighthouse. The echo of his footsteps faded quickly into the dark.

CHAPTER FOUR

Something was wrong. Darrell could feel it in her gut and in her head. The trip had taken too long, for one thing. She tried to collect her whirling thoughts, but it was impossible to think when her head throbbed with every heartbeat. She reached a hand up to touch a spot behind her ear. Her hair felt matted and wet, and nausea coursed through her again. So it *was* worse than usual. This time she'd been hurt.

She remembered Kate's hand on her arm and the fleeting sight of Brodie grabbing Kate's shoulder. The yank that had pulled her into the maelstrom was unforgettable; her bones still ached from it. And strange as they were, these memories allowed her the comfort of familiarity. But something was still different.

She slipped a peppermint into her mouth and paused a moment as the hot sweetness curled around her tongue.

First things first. Where was she now? Moving with care, she slowly sat up.

It was half-dark, and the air smelled musty. Well, that wasn't so bad. Her first journey had landed her in a cave that was blacker than pitch and she'd survived all right. Nothing could be worse than that first trip into darkness and fear.

Could it?

The velvet touch of dog fur was fresh on her fingers, but when she tentatively stretched out and felt around, Delaney wasn't within reach.

That was it. Delaney had been with her in the tunnel under the school — but now she was alone. Darrell stopped moving and listened carefully. No sound of the dog's hearty, happy breathing. No sound at all. The air felt heavy and close, and …

What was that?

Her heart settled back down in her chest. Only the sound of a drop of water, splashing.

Splashing where? Into what?

Darrell drew her legs into her chest. Her hand crept down to her right knee, and the unmistakeable feel of coarse cloth bound to heavy wood brought her whirling thoughts into focus; an unaccountable excitement fluttered in her stomach.

It's happened again …

The last thing she remembered was walking with her

friends through the hidden passage leading out of the Eagle Glen library. But where on earth had she ended up? And *when*?

She rubbed her eyes and tried to push the headache away through sheer force of will. As always, the peppermint helped a little with the nausea, but she knew nothing but time would quiet the pain. She gathered up a handful of sleeve and pressed it to the tender spot behind her ear. The pain was still intense, but the wound did not seem to be actively bleeding, and that had to be a good thing.

Using her hands as support, she crab-walked sideways until she could feel a solid stone wall at her shoulder. Cold slipped through seams and folds of her clothing, and she hugged herself for warmth. The mint in her mouth melted away as she leaned against the wall with a sigh and tried to figure out how she had come to be here and what exactly was to be done next.

She seemed to be in the middle of some kind of long passage or hall, but it was clearly not the dusty passage underneath the school. The air smelled different — of seaweed and fish underlined with a sweet, rotten stench she did not want to put a name to.

Which way to turn? Darrell flipped a mental coin and looked to the right. "Seems as good a direction as any," she muttered.

Using the wall for balance, Darrell pulled herself upright. Her right leg was heavy, and the act of walking no longer came naturally. She slid one hand along the clammy surface of the rock and stepped cautiously down the passageway to the right. The air still felt dank, but the hint of an icy breeze stirred the damp hairs on her neck. Feeling more confident in her choice, she moved instinctively toward the breath of air. The footing was treacherous, and Darrell found herself wishing for the carved walking stick that had once been a gift from an old man in Florence. Limping, she felt the stone surface rough under her fingertips, and she followed the wall down the passage.

Most worrisome was the absence of her friends and Delaney. She could still feel the way his fur had bunched under his collar like a ruff as she'd held him last. He had to be here somewhere — but she did not know enough about her surroundings to risk calling out to him. Not yet.

And what about Brodie and Kate? They'd been in the passage with her ... She stopped suddenly. Brodie and Kate had been there — they'd all been there — because of Paris. Darrell quailed inwardly. What if she'd dragged Paris into this, too?

A new sense of panic pushing her forward, Darrell followed the passage around a slight curve and noticed the dark had lifted a little, though no source of light could be seen. In the low, greenish glow she could see what she had only been able to feel before. Her twenty-first-century outfit of jeans and a sweater was gone. She was now wearing a long, free-flowing skirt of heavy wool under a decorative overskirt with a pattern lost in the dim light. The package of mints in her pocket had disappeared, leaving a few loose candies. And all that remained of the art pencil she always carried in the back pocket of her jeans was a stick of charcoal with a jagged end.

And most significant of all, of course, was her right foot. Darrell sighed and raised her leg awkwardly. No state-of-the-art prosthesis to be seen. In its place was a roughly foot-shaped contraption carved out of heavy reddish wood and hinged at the spot where her ankle would be — if she still had one.

Darrell sighed and pressed onward. The new foot swung clumsily, but it allowed her to keep moving, and that was what she needed most right now.

The rough wall that she had been relying upon for balance carried on a few feet more and then dipped sharply into a niche. Near the floor, emerging from the solid rock, was a tiny stone altar. Below it a small basin scooped into the cobbled floor.

Darrell's running shoe had become a soft leather slipper on her left foot. This allowed her to walk very quietly, but the rustle of her skirts and the clatter of her wooden foot was still noise enough to send a mouse scampering away from the face of the altar. She stopped for a moment to watch the creature skitter down the hall and melt into the darkness, then she dropped to kneel near the tiny structure. Perhaps it held a clue to her whereabouts.

A trickle of water ran from a flower-shaped stone spigot partway up the wall and dripped lazily into a stone basin, green and white with lime deposits and age. So this was what had drawn the mouse.

A small collection of objects rested on the stone shelf. A couple of leather-bound books, an assortment of three or four scrolls of heavy paper or parchment and —

A menorah.

Her fingers traced the Hebrew letters and symbols etched into the heavy brass base. She scraped her nail above one symbol and a fine layer of yellow wax curled and dropped into the shadows.

"*Deus Do Elogio*! What are you doing here? This is no safe place for a young woman."

The voice was gentle, but Darrell was no less startled for it. Her hands flew away from the items on the stone altar as she scrambled to stand. The menorah teetered dangerously on the edge of the shelf, but before Darrell could move to save it she felt the brush of a warm hand and the menorah was safely back in its place.

"Is it time to celebrate Chanukah?" Darrell blurted.

The man beside her was hooded and in the dim light she could not see his face. He folded his hands together inside the heavy sleeves of his robe. "This candlestick belonged once to a man I knew long ago. And yes, during the Festival of Lights it is sometimes used for its proper function, but these days it is mostly a provider of much-needed light for travellers such as yourself." He paused. "You know of this festival," he added quietly. "You are of the *Sephardim?*"

Darrell shook her head, unsure how much to reveal. "No — no. At least I don't think so. It's just — well — I know a man who is Jewish. He has a menorah a bit like this one."

The hooded man shifted, and though she could make out no other detail, Darrell could see the gleam of his eyes as he scrutinized her face. "I was not told to expect a traveller," he said, as though to himself. He walked over to the low stone altar and knelt for a moment.

Darrell stood uneasily against one wall, not knowing whether to move on or stay. After a long moment, the man crossed himself and stood up. "I came here to take away these things," he said. "This place is no longer safe. But instead of just collecting a few religious relics, I now find I have a young girl to spirit away as well."

He looked at her critically. "I see you walk with a limp," he said, pointing to her foot. His eyes softened. "You have suffered much, and there will be more ahead, I fear."

"Please, sir," Darrell's desperation welled up inside her and right out of her mouth, "I have been travelling with some friends, and I've — I have somehow managed to lose them. Have you seen them anywhere? They should be nearby — two boys and a girl, about my height?"

He picked up the menorah and slipped it into a cloth bag with the other items. "I think you had best follow me, *Señhorita*," he said quietly. "Through chance or good fortune you have stumbled upon the one person in this place who will do you no harm. The days are no longer safe for open travel, but I can at least guarantee you sanctuary until I locate your friends and move you safely on your way."

He pointed down the corridor and took her arm in what seemed a polite gesture. Darrell swallowed tightly and hurried along beside him, his hand on her arm firm evidence that at this moment, she had little other choice.

The familiar burn settled deep into Darrell's leg as the hooded man hustled her along the corridor. There was no time to talk, no time to worry that she was being rushed along by a man who looked like he had walked off the cover of a book still sitting unread in her pack at school. She needed all her powers of concentration not to slip on the damp cobblestones.

Shortly after taking her arm, the man paused long enough to heave open a stout wooden door, banded with iron, that appeared in the gloom of the passageway. She could hear the sound of rushing water somewhere in the distance. The door led into a slightly less gloomy corridor, with torches that flared and flickered at intervals along the wall. Darrell noted with a pang of worry as the door swung silently back into place that it was faced with plaster and fitted so tightly into the wall that the cracks indicating its presence were barely evident in the gloom. Even the ring used to pull it open was recessed into the wall and would be just another lump in the plaster to an unobservant passerby.

"Keep sharp your eyes," he whispered, "for if your *companheiros* are here without guidance, they may be lost to us forever."

Darrell staggered, and the man tightened his hold on her arm. "You are in pain?" he asked kindly.

She shook her head, misery clogging her throat like a gag. *Give your head a shake*, she thought. *Feeling sorry for yourself is not going to help find your friends.*

To take her mind off her fears, she stole a sideways glance at her companion in the flickering torchlight. He wore a long robe of heavy grey wool under an open cloak of the same fabric. The robe was tied at the waist by a rough length of rope, from one end of which dangled an iron ring of keys that clanked against his leg as he walked. The only concession to decoration was tucked into the rope at his waist. Darrell recognized the polished stones and small golden crucifix of a rosary. He must be was a priest, then. But a priest with a menorah? Darrell's head buzzed with unanswered questions. She wished desperately that she'd taken the time to read Uncle Frank's book or had listened even a little to the new teacher's droning history lessons at school.

The man showed no further inclination towards speech but walked swiftly with his reluctant charge. As they hurried along one corridor after another she puzzled over the language he spoke. *We spoke*, she thought, for she had conversed with him as readily as if it had been her native tongue. Not Spanish, as she'd taken an introductory course at school last year. And yet — he'd called her *Señhorita* ...

The air began to feel fresher, but the hall was still clammy, and Darrell tucked her free hand into her long sleeve. They followed a path she couldn't hope to remember. First a left, then two rights and up a twisted spiral stair. Spiderwebs clung in every crevice, and the gritty floor showed no evidence of regular use, let alone cleaning. Darrell was convinced the passage doubled back on itself several times, and she tried to recognize repeating landmarks. Hadn't she seen that particular torch before? And what about that bit of broken plaster?

After ten minutes or so her muscles began to loosen as she picked up the rhythm of walking on the new wooden foot. She'd been forced in the past to walk on little more than a stick of wood, so this was almost easy by comparison. She was just mustering the breath to ask a question when her companion came to an abrupt halt at yet another heavy wooden door.

Darrell was relieved to see that this door was not camouflaged in any way. In fact, it seemed quite recognizable. A large crest was carved into the middle, the design an intricate cruciform surrounded by roaring lions raised high on their hind legs. He selected a single key from the jangling bunch at his waist and turned it in the large iron lock.

With a mighty heave, the grey-robed friar pulled the heavy door open and courteously held it while she stepped inside. He followed behind, and, leaving the portal slightly ajar, he faced her and pulled back his hood at last. Gentle brown eyes gazed at Darrell from a weathered face. His hair was straight and iron grey, and the hair on top of his head had been shaved off in a neat circle.

"I apologize for the hurry, *Señhorita*, but it is imperative I keep you from prying eyes until we are safely away from this place."

Darrell looked nervously around the small room. Her heart sank a little. No sign of her friends anywhere. "Safely away? From where — where are we?"

"We are far from the grotto, *Señhorita*," he said. His voice was low and urgent. "Not a soul save myself knows the route we followed today. For your own safety I must insist you remain here. I beg of you to forget all that you saw in that place. In these uncertain times, it is best that some things remain unsaid."

"But ..." Questions surged to her lips, fighting for precedence. "Do you know how I came here?"

He shook his head firmly. "Nor do I want to. The less we all know in truth means fewer people meet untimely deaths." His voice dropped to a whisper. "I desire no further blood on my hands."

She pushed the fear that his words awoke in her aside and clutched at his sleeve. "I must find my friends," she said quickly. "A tall boy and a girl with red hair. There may be a second boy, with — with blonde hair. I lost them just before I met you."

He looked horrified. "Near the grotto? I fear I mis-understood you earlier. This is terrible news, *Señhorita*. If your associates wander freely around the fortress a soldier — or worse, a priest — could find them at any time. I must try to locate them at once."

Darrell could hear her pulse pounding in her ears. "Thank you, sir. You cannot possibly know how impor-tant it is for me to find them." She paused. "I have been travelling some distance, *Señhor*," she managed. "Please tell me — where is this place?"

He touched a finger to the side of his nose and smiled briefly. "Do not fear, my child. You are safe here for the present. We are in the monastery near to the Lisboa Cathedral, in the centre of the most powerful nation in the world. I will return shortly to bring you news of your friends and to reunite you with your people. *Adeus.*" The door closed behind him quietly, but the click of the bolt sliding home echoed like a death knell.

Safe she might be, but what she had feared most as she hurried through the labyrinth below had come to pass — she was a prisoner.

After taking five long, shaky breaths to calm her nerves, Darrell slipped over to the door of the room and tried it. The handle was an iron ring that did not turn, and the lock was so solid the door would not even rattle on its hinges.

Despair washed over her, and she slumped onto the small cot pushed against one wall. This was unlike any journey she had ever taken. Her friends were missing — Delaney was missing.

"Let's hope I am the only one who is truly missing," she said aloud.

Judging by the light from the high window, dusk was gathering. A cool breeze whirled in through the unglazed opening and the room held a deep chill. No shutters stood ready to guard against drafts, but they would have been useless anyway, as the window was far too high on the wall to reach.

The friar had left a small fire burning in the grate near the door to her room, and she added more fuel from the pile of wood and charcoal nearby. She pulled a worn woollen blanket from the bed and wrapped herself in it, kneeling as close to the fire as she could manage. It was time to think — not that she had much else to do.

One side of her roasted while the other froze, and yet Darrell suspected her surroundings had been designed to allow the resident some comfort. She looked around in the dancing light of the fire. The tiny room had a straw mattress raised off the floor on a wooden bedstead and a small wooden desk and chair. There was the coarsely woven blanket she had taken from the bed, and the straw in the mattress was fresh and fragrant. The priest had left behind precious wood for the fire. Remembering the dried dung that fuelled medieval fires made her grateful for the clean smell of fruit wood burning in the grate.

Under the desk was a wide-mouthed china bowl that Darrell recognized with some trepidation as a chamber pot. Ugh. And yet, these surroundings would probably be considered luxurious by most Portuguese standards of the day. But what did she know of Portuguese standards?

"And what day?" she muttered aloud. "*When* am I?"

Everything inside her rebelled at the thought of just sitting and awaiting her fate. She rose again to prowl the tiny space. Above her head a glimpse of sky pinkened into sunset.

"Too bad I don't have any of Brodie's climbing gear," she muttered. "I could be out that window in two minutes flat."

But climbing gear was not at hand. Darrell flopped on the bed and tugged her heavy skirts up over her knees. The evidence was inarguable. It was time to face facts.

She gazed down at her legs stretched out on the bed in front of her. This morning when she had dressed for school, she had donned jeans, a heavy sweater layered over a T-shirt, and a pair of running shoes. Now she looked down at one long, lean limb, clad in some kind of woollen stocking and shod in a leather slipper. The other was red with cold and bare to below the knee, where it was wrapped tightly in cloth and attached to a leg with a jointed ankle and simple wooden foot.

Darrell ran her hand over the surface of this strange contraption. More than anything, the feel of the smooth wood under her fingers proved the inevitable. It had happened again.

She was lost, somewhere in time.

The sound of chanting voices snapped Darrell out of her reverie. A heavy scent wafted in through the high window, and it took a moment or two to place it. Incense.

She looked around the room again. Spartan, clean, with space for little more than sleep and quiet contemplation. A friar's humble cell. And locked inside — a prisoner from another time and place.

The voices, borne on the wind, rose and fell in rhythmic chanting. Darrell knew at once that she was listening to Latin, and yet the strange ability to speak the vernacular of this earlier time didn't stretch her ability to understand. She listened as the voices echoed, dolorous through the dark. Something skittered at her window above. A bird? A bat? At this lonely time, Darrell would have welcomed any company at all. She curled into her thin blanket and fell asleep thinking about her dog.

The thin blanket was not much help against the biting wind blowing through the open window, but it was all Darrell had and she was grateful for its warmth. How long had she slept? The fire had long ago burned low, the pile of wood and coal soon gone. The people of this time must really have to work to stay warm.

Darrell shivered. It was becoming painfully clear that function dictated fashion. Even with all the layers of clothing she found herself wearing, she still thought enviously back to the heavy woollen robes worn by the friar, her captor.

Her captor — where was he? Twice over the course of the long, frigid night she had heard scurrying noises in the hall outside her door. Raised voices and running feet, but no sound of a sliding bolt. What if he never returned?

A gentle tapping sound made her raise her head sharply, but after a moment she realized that the noise came from outside. Rain had started to fall. Not quite snow, in spite of the cold. Bone chilling didn't even begin to describe it. Darrell's fingers ached with it, her feet had gone numb from it, and her brain felt rattled from all the trembling.

A few drops pattered onto the stone windowsill and slid down the walls along cracks and fissures in the rock. Darrell curled up as tightly as she could manage on the straw mattress, tucking the thin blanket carefully around her cold foot. Fear that had sprouted in the dark was wrapping its tiny, fast-growing vines around the edges of her conscious thought. Unable to sleep again, she slipped into a reverie, listening for the sound of freedom but hearing only rain.

Even without the fear, the cold was bad. Bad enough to kill? Darrell had read in her *National Geographic* magazines of how freezing was supposed to be a gentle way to die. You warm up by the end, the stories said. You just go peacefully to sleep and then stay that way. Well, if that was the case, she must have a way to go yet. This cold *hurt*.

She looked around the tiny stone cell. No food. And worse, the small clay jug of sweetened water stood long empty. Perhaps since the cold hadn't yet managed to kill her, fear might just step in and finish the job.

Some of the *National Geographic* types had drunk their own urine when their water ran out.

That got her moving. She staggered to her feet and started pacing, six strides one way, seven the other. "Disgusting," she said aloud. "If I ever make it home, I am cancelling that subscription."

The wooden prosthesis creaked a little as she paced, and though the space was small, she worked hard to master the knack of walking with it. Instead of the peg she had been forced to wear on previous journeys, this foot actually resembled its function. The wood was somewhat roughly shaped and the approximation looked more like a boot than a foot, but it was stiffly jointed at the ankle and sanded smooth where it was bound to her leg — both vast improvements on past incarnations.

She peered up at the minute patch of sky she could see through the window. Pale pink dawn had given way to a thin winter blue tinged with grey. And the air smelled so cold — perhaps it would snow. "That'll finish me for sure," she muttered.

Anxiety had kept her quiet when she'd heard the night-muffled voices outside her cell. Now thirst and cold drove past her fear, and she pounded against the door, crying out for help.

Nothing.

She was falling, falling.

Time had swept her up once more and she twisted and whirled, no control of arms or legs, her head snapping backwards. She awoke with a jerk to the sound of the scrape of metal on wood. Hunger and crying had finally given way to exhaustion, and Darrell had fallen asleep stretched uncomfortably sideways across the straw mattress. Befuddled by her dream and sore from sleeping without removing the wooden leg, she took a moment to remember where she was. The darkness of the room was complete, and the open door showed no light from the hall. The rain had stopped, and a thin white sliver of moon gave only enough light for Darrell to make out the shape of a person standing over her in the darkness.

"Whazt?" she managed blearily.

"*Silêncio!* If you value your life, speak not a word," a voice breathed in her ear.

Darrell hurriedly pushed her foot into the soft leather shoe and stood uncertainly beside the bed. Night had come again, but it no longer mattered. Her lips were cracked with thirst and her body felt stiff with cold, but the sight of the open door was so welcome adrenaline surged through her. She felt as though she could run for miles.

She watched as the priest slid open the single wooden drawer and rummaged through it. Suddenly, he dropped to his knees and reached so far back that he had to crawl almost completely underneath. Darrell heard the man mutter something under his breath. She took an uncertain step toward the open door. What to do — run or speak? After a moment she settled on the latter.

"Uh — do you need help with anything?" she whispered, feeling foolish.

He lifted his head to reply and banged it hard on the open desk drawer. As he cried out, the desk creaked and a wooden panel shot out from underneath and hit the floor with a clatter. Darrell could hear the sound of a number of objects falling.

"I'm so sorry," she whispered, bending over to help.

"No time — no time," he gasped, scrambling to pick up the fallen objects. A trickle of blood trailed into the corner of the priest's eye.

"You're hurt," she protested.

"It matters not, *Señhorita*," he said. He brushed the blood away impatiently, smearing it across one cheek. "I am terribly sorry to have left you here so long, but there was no help for it. We must away," he continued. "These artifacts cannot be found here —"

He reached inside one of his voluminous sleeves and pulled out a rough cloth bag into which he stuffed the various objects that had fallen from the drawer.

"Found?" Darrell was curious. "By whom?"

He shook his head impatiently and thrust the menorah and a few small, more regularly shaped packages into the bag.

"*Señhorita*, the little time we have has almost flown," he said, his voice low and urgent. "You must place your faith in *nosso Deus* and hold tight to his servant for there is no time for further explanation," he said, tucking her hand firmly into the crook of his arm.

Darrell nodded. Her head spun a little from the time she had spent without food or water, but a surge of energy coursed through her at the chance to get away. "My friends?" she whispered. "I mentioned them to you before."

He nodded briefly. "Rest easy, *Señhorita*. I have located your three friends," he said, his voice low. "And I aim to reunite you as soon as I am able. But for now we must fly."

Three? Darrell's stomach clenched again. So Paris had been pulled through time with them, after all. *I'll get him back safely,* she vowed. *I won't let everything that took place with Conrad happen again.*

They slipped into the empty passageway, while around them muffled sounds of movement seemed everywhere; shouts and whispers echoed in the sinuous space. Darrell had only taken a few steps down the hall when her companion stopped without warning and knelt at her feet. Darrell stood frozen to the spot, not sure what to do. She felt a tug on her wooden foot and realized that it was being bound with some kind of soft fabric.

Sure enough, as they started to move again, any sound made by the wood striking the floor of the stone passageway was dampened by the new binding.

Without advantage of a torch or even a candle, Darrell clutched the arm of her rescuer and stumbled along as best she could. The ground was terribly uneven. She smiled a little, glad for the practice she'd had walking on this new wooden foot with its jointed ankle. Now tightly bound in cloth, the ankle had lost some of its mobility, but any creakiness was muffled as well.

Twisting and turning through a series of tunnels, Darrell concentrated on keeping upright and quiet. For what seemed like hours the friar made no sound but hurried along with one hand held lightly to the wall and the other clutching Darrell's arm. Suddenly he stopped short, and Darrell found herself unceremoniously pushed against the cold stone wall.

"Be still," he hissed. Darrell, heart pounding, did her best to comply.

A door creaked, and her companion gave a sharp intake of breath. Moonlight, bright as day after the stygian tunnels, poured in molten silver through the open doorway.

Darrell felt the breath of his voice once more in her ear. "Stay close beside me. We must melt into the shadows."

She nodded, and they slipped through the stone doorway into the chill night.

Not a single tree or bush grew near enough to the portal to offer any protection in the clear moonlight. The fingernail moon cast weird shadows through the wind-strewn branches of a large tree that grew at some distance from the door, and it was toward the tree that they hurried. Turning for a look at the building that held her captive so long, she watched too late as the heavy door from which they had emerged swung free, pushed by a gust of wind. The door slammed with a bang.

"*Alto ai!*" The voice came from somewhere outside the door and above. Darrell thought her heart would freeze in her chest.

Her companion pulled Darrell into the shadow behind the broad trunk of the tree and swore quietly. "We are undone."

Darrell raised her eyebrows. No ordinary priest, this.

A crash of armoured feet mingled with yelling voices. Light blazed as a dozen or more torches were raised on the parapet of what Darrell could now see was an old fort or castle. Among the soldiers, a figure in a scarlet cloak appeared and leaned over the edge to peer down into the trees.

The friar's hood fell back as he clutched Darrell by both shoulders and the moon gleamed off the pale skin of his tonsured scalp. "Do you think you can run on that contraption? It is our only hope." He gestured at the wooden foot.

Darrell felt numb to fear — there was nothing that would make her return to the cell. "Just watch me," she said, teeth clenched so they wouldn't chatter.

"Then let us see if we can make it a race."

He yanked up his hood and took Darrell's hand, pulling her around the back of the heavy trunk. Hand in hand, they bolted down an icy path.

CHAPTER FIVE

Running.

Slowing in an effort to haul more cold air into already burning lungs and then running again. Tree branches whipping her face. Countless stumbles, three bad falls, and Darrell still didn't know who she was running from. All she knew was that she did not want to go back to the cell. The air outside was cold, but it tasted of freedom and was enough to give her tired limbs the strength to push on a little farther. Mostly she ran, clutching tightly to her companion's hand, with little time to wonder about anything but where her next breath was coming from. The treed area around the fortress had quickly given way to tightly crowded buildings and homes, and they ran through the dark streets of a city asleep.

If Darrell had felt lost in the underground passage she was positively baffled now as they wove in and among lanes so narrow that in many cases they were forced to run single-file. The air had a rank, stale odour, as if no wind was strong enough to blow the smell of humanity away. The footing was uneven, and Darrell was glad of the dark because she did not want to see some of the things she knew she'd stepped in. Houses and buildings gave way to lean-tos and shanties and then back to large houses again. In this night, black as a raven's wing, it was hard to distinguish one building from another. Most of the doorways they passed were barred and dark, but the occasional gleam of light through a shutter was apparently enough to allow the priest to find his way through the tortuous route.

A new smell floated in on the fetid air, and Darrell's head snapped up in alarm.

Fire.

Something was burning — something big.

Sounds of pursuit had long faded into the distance, and Darrell was about to gasp out her need for a rest when the priest stopped running and slipped through the open doorway of a small cottage.

The place was empty, though a low fire burned in a central pit on the floor. The priest closed the door behind Darrell and dropped a heavy beam into the scarred wooden supports on either side.

He smiled at her grimly. "You must not be fooled by the present lack of pursuit," he said quietly. "The Dominican brothers have been making speeches in the market today, and I fear they will stir the rabble against your people. And I do not like the smell of the fire in the air. Anything more than the whiff of small kitchen fires is unnatural at night and brings fear into my heart. It is imperative to keep you away from public view just now. I must leave now to fetch your friends."

Relief coursed through her again. "Are they nearby?"

He nodded. "One of my — colleagues — took them for beggars when they were found wandering outside the Tower of Belem. It would seem they worried as much for you as you do for them. But I must leave explanations for another time. The Jewish population of the city is being gathered together, and I fear the worst."

"Who *are* you?" she asked curiously.

"It is better that you not learn my true name," he replied. "But you must know that I am sworn to keep you safe as I am able until it is possible to get you over the border and into Spain."

"Spain?" Darrell began to feel lost again. And yet — perhaps this was where Gramps's lessons came in. She ventured a guess. "How can it be safe there? What about the Inquisition?"

The priest stepped quietly over to the single window and peered outside before shutting and barring it as tightly as the door.

"Spain is much calmer these days now that Torquemada has been dead these seven or eight years," he said quietly. "And as you must know, the Inquisition has been in abeyance here in Portugal under King Manuel."

Well, I know now, thought Darrell, with some satisfaction that her guess had proved right.

"He is a just man," the priest continued, "though I suspect he values the physical properties of the Jewish community more than their spiritual souls. Still, I fear the Dominican thirst for blood will rise once more. You may not know that before he was the Spanish queen's personal priest, Tomás de Torquemada was a member of the Dominican order. And here in Portugal, even though his influence has passed, they are relentless in routing out *conversos*." He folded his arms into his sleeves. "Our escape from the fortress did not go unnoticed."

"But I keep trying to tell you," Darrell protested, "I'm not Jewish. Why would the Dominicans care about me?"

He raised his eyebrows. "You need make no denials to me, *Señhorita*," he said gently. "I have been finding sanctuary and a means of escape for members of your faith for many years, since even before the Inquisition took hold in Spain." He smiled. "If you are not Jewish, how did you find your way to the grotto? It has been my primary meeting spot for *conversos* for the past several years."

Darrell struggled to find an answer. "I cannot really explain," she said at last.

He wiped his hand across his forehead. "And I do not want you to, *menina*. Nothing is safe these days." He looked at her piercingly. "Even if, as you say, you are not Jewish, anything that connects you with those who facilitate escape for others puts you at risk." He gestured at the cloth bag. "Before you on that table is evidence enough to ensure us both a trip into the flames."

"What kind of priests burn people to death?" whispered Darrell.

The old man looked incredulous. "It is common knowledge that the Holy See has granted the Inquisition power to impose the ultimate sacrifice on unbelievers," he said. "Torquemada said it first: 'Convert, leave, or die.' His idea of the route to heaven was often through the flames. Since the great Spanish expulsion, Jews have come to Portugal for sanctuary, but I am afraid those days are over. The route east across the water to Turkey is the safest now, in spite of the small dangers provided by pirates and their ilk."

"I have never thought of pirates as being a small danger," said Darrell.

The priest laughed bitterly. "Compared to the dangers to those not baptized into the Catholic Church, pirates are as fearsome as a child's doll," he said. "My own brethren, the Franciscans, believe that fire purifies the soul. The Dominicans and priests of other orders share those beliefs. And those who will not recant their heathenish ways must burn."

"But why are you different?" asked Darrell. "Why aren't you out collecting victims for the new Portuguese Inquisition? You are a member of the Catholic faith."

He smiled gently and gestured towards the doorway. "I have tarried too long already and to answer your questions would delay me even further. I must send word that Lisboa is no longer safe for those seeking sanctuary from the Inquisition," he said. "I promise to return as soon as I am able, and I will try to help you understand a little more at that time."

"But what about my friends?" Darrell asked, stalling.

"Soon enough," he replied. "I must go." The priest leaned toward the table and collected a small tallow candle that he quickly lit. He rummaged in the cloth bag and removed the menorah, slipping the candle into one of the slots. He clasped one of her hands in his own and looked at her closely. "Perhaps the story you have told me is true and perhaps not. You certainly seem unlike any young woman I have met before. However, it matters not at all — I would still see to your safety." He smiled wryly. "I am sure my Jewish friends, be they your people or not, will forgive our use of their menorah. They would understand your need for a light in the darkness." He wrapped the remaining items in the cloth bag and tucked it under Darrell's arm.

Darrell clutched it tightly. "I'll bar the door behind you," she said, "but how will I know when you return with my friends?"

He knocked swiftly on the tabletop — two sharp raps and one long. "This will be my sign. Do not open the door to any voice but my own, and if you hear soldiers, climb through the window and take refuge on the roof. They haven't time to search every rooftop, and there is no other place to hide." He pointed at a sideboard. "Please refresh yourself and eat. There is sweet water, bread, and cheese. I will return as soon as I am able."

Darrell slid the heavy beam across the door as it closed behind the priest and drank deeply from the pitcher on the table before sitting down to wait. Though it was still only an hour or two after midnight, noises and shouting came from near and far as the city roused around her. The smell of smoke was pervasive, and she could hear voices from the surrounding houses raised in concern.

She put another small piece of wood on the central fire in the cottage and sat down at the table, making short work of the bread and the piece of hard cheese the priest had left under a linen cloth.

Stomach full for what seemed the first time in days, she walked over to stand beside the shuttered window.

Resting her face against the rough wood, Darrell could peer through a large knothole for a view out front. People were on the streets now, some running, others walking; almost all headed for an area behind the cottage and out of Darrell's visual range. She watched, barely breathing, searching for her friends and the only man who could bring them their freedom.

Vermilion dawn streaked the sky, and Darrell found herself close to panic. She pried her eye from the knothole and paced the room in an effort to both keep warm and decide what to do next. Soldiers were now marching through the streets, and it seemed that the whole city had come awake. Whatever was happening was spreading like wildfire, perhaps literally.

She held her small candle aloft and looked around. The floor was just tamped earth but was clean-swept and free of the straw and rushes that so often harboured fleas and disease. Darrell sank down on to the stool and gazed at the back wall of the room. It was fitted with shelves, each heavily laden with clay jars and baskets.

Looking for something to take her mind from her fears, she shook the contents of the priest's bag onto the rough tabletop. "He didn't say I couldn't look," she muttered. Inside the bag were two leather-bound volumes — one large and heavy, the other smaller. The first proved to be a ledger with pages of row upon row of letters and numbers written in a neat and careful hand. Darrell found it completely indecipherable.

"Not exactly a John Grisham," she said dejectedly.

The second book looked less promising still. It was small and very worn — little more than a notebook with a creased and heavily water-stained cover of russet leather.

She flipped it open anyway and was rewarded with more of the same. The first several pages overflowed with neat rows of letters, singly and in pairs, though this time the entries appeared to be dated. Darrell traced her finger along the rows for several pages, speculating idly.

Letters — consonants and vowels both, but no words. Always in pairs — initials, perhaps? A code? Whatever it was, it worked, because Darrell could make nothing of it after half an hour.

She closed the book and went to return the ledgers to the bag when the back cover of the smaller book snagged on a rough board from the tabletop.

Inside the back cover were more letters, but this time not only in pairs. Words. The handwriting near the start was the same as that in the ledger lists, but after a page or two, a new handwriting began. Curious, Darrell drew the candle closer, tracing the letters with one finger.

The words seemed strangely shaped and yet familiar somehow ...

She scrabbled in the pocket of her skirt. After a moment her fingers closed on the broken stick of charcoal that she had found in her pocket near the grotto. She flipped open the larger ledger and ripped a blank page out of the back. The candle burned lower, but daylight was starting to creep through the cracks in the shutters.

Darrell bent her head began to transpose the letters carefully on to the scrap of paper. Her writing grew more feverish with every word.

After a time, writer's cramp knotted her hand and she looked up with alarm at the nearly guttering candle. Full daylight was evident outside the shutters now, so she let the candle burn itself out. Rubbing her hand, she held her tattered page to the light and began to read aloud.

Darrell had managed to read only two or three of the sentences transcribed from the back of the small book when there was a sudden pounding on the door. It was definitely not the priest's secret knock.

"*Abra! Abra a porta!*"

Darrell jumped up with the ledgers in her hands. After what she had just read she could not bear to throw them in the fire, and the leather covers would not burn in any case. She looked around desperately for a hiding place.

"In the name of the king, we demand entrance!"
Another resounding crash on the door. Darrell
wrapped the ledgers hurriedly in the cloth bag and
jammed them behind a large clay jar of pickled fish.
A third crash splintered one of the boards in the
door, and Darrell could see a face looking through
the crack.

"*Marranos!*" roared a voice and a hand punched
through the splintered board of the doorway. "Swine!"

Darrell realized too late that all the exits to the
small cottage were at the front. She stood beside the
table, waiting for the final blow to fall. Instead a quiet
voice crept through the cracked and broken door.

"*Tem calma meu, amigo.* Calm down, my friend."

The priest!

The rasping voice that had shouted though the door
took on a sudden obsequious tone. "*Mil perdões*, Father.
We were told this place was a secret sty for *marranos*."

"A forgivable error, my friend, considering the part
of the city," said the priest. "But there are no Jewish people here. This is the humble abode of my dear departed
aunt, with only her daughter, *minha prima*, inside."

"Rosita!" Darrell could see the Franciscan's face as
he called out through the cracked door. "Rosita *minha
querida*, there is no need to be afraid. Open the door
and I will show this good fellow that those whom he
seeks are not to be found here."

Darrell hurried to the door and lifted the heavy board. Without the support of the bar the rest of the door collapsed under its own weight in a shower of splinters.

The Franciscan friar stepped in over the splinters and motioned inside. "You see? Only *minha prima*, my young cousin."

The soldier stepped into the room. His armour was tarnished and soot-stained, and Darrell was surprised at his tiny stature. His voice had sounded much bigger through the door. However, her eyes were torn from the soldier by the two figures standing behind him. She flew through the door and into Kate's arms. Brodie squeezed her shoulder reassuringly, and Delaney wagged happily at her side.

"I can't believe you are safe," said Darrell, blinking back tears of relief.

"Don't say a word," whispered Kate. "We've got to get out of here *now*."

The friar slapped the soldier on the back and smiled serenely. "Go ahead, look around. You will see all is well."

Darrell widened her eyes at the Franciscan and he moved gently to her side. "The bag is behind the jar of fish on the wall," she hissed. "I didn't have time to hide it anywhere else."

He nodded and said in a loud voice. "You must run to the market for me, my dear. I remember now that I am quite out of wine, and my good friend here may need to pause in his labours and share a glass with me." In a low voice he added, "Pay close heed to your sister and her good husband. They know the way."

Darrell nodded and then watched in horror as the soldier picked up the menorah from where it sat, with its single stub of a candle, right in the middle of the table.

"Off you go, my dears," the priest said, and he gave Darrell's arm a quick squeeze before he pushed her away. He turned back to the soldier.

"I see you have found that old candlestick. It was a gift from my ..."

Brodie grabbed Darrell's arm, and she found herself being hustled up the street with Kate on her other side and Delaney at their heels. The roads were full of men and soldiers running. A few children skipped alongside the soldiers but most clung to their mothers' skirts in the shadows of darkened doorways. It was hard to read the atmosphere — part celebration, part mob action. There was no time to stop and find out more.

"It's only a short way from here," gasped Brodie. He held Darrell firmly under her right arm. Her feet were practically skimming the rocky surface of the road as she ran along between her two friends. "Unfortunately, it's straight uphill."

"Everywhere is straight uphill in Lisbon," panted Kate. "There are seven of them right here in the centre of the city."

The miasma of burning was all about them, and Darrell could see the flames in a nearby square. There was no time or breath left for speech as they climbed the steep slope towards an enormous castle that over-looked the city.

Kate's face was ashen in spite of the run. "Whatever you do," she said, "don't look at the fires."

Darrell nodded and concentrated on following Delaney. His once-golden fur was smudged and sooty, but there was no mistaking his energy. He wore a rough knotted rope around his neck and dashed around them to lead the way up the hill with Darrell and her friends in close pursuit. The castle gate was a scene of further chaos. People ran in all directions, uncertainty and even panic written across many faces. Delaney veered around the side of the castle wall and stopped, panting, near a guardhouse. Kate dropped her skirts and put her hands on her knees, gasping for breath.

Brodie stuck his head into the guardhouse. "Looks like they've all gone to the burning," he said grimly. He rested his hand on Darrell's shoulder. "Are you really okay?" he asked.

"Yeah." Darrell nodded. "I have so much to tell you. Is there somewhere safe we can go and talk?"

"No," said Kate, her voice tinged with panic. "The Dominicans have rounded up all the Jewish people in Lisbon. They're going to kill them all, Darrell. Your priest is the only person we've met who listens to reason, which means he'll probably be dead before the day is over. We must leave *now*."

"But, just a minute, you two, I think I may have found—"

"I'm sorry Darrell, but it doesn't matter what you've found," interrupted Brodie. "Kate is right. We have to go."

Delaney barked sharply, and the trio looked up to see a line of soldiers marching purposefully towards them. In the lead was the soldier who had broken down the cottage door. Clutched securely in the arms of two others was the Franciscan priest.

"*Marranos!*" screamed the first soldier, and the group broke ranks and ran up the slope towards the castle wall.

"*Go!*" Brodie pushed Darrell into the guardhouse. Pieces of armour were strewn about haphazardly as though they had been recently discarded. A passageway led from the guardhouse into the gate yard outside, guarded by an enormous portcullis. Darrell started for the passageway, but Kate pulled her back.

"No — this way!"

In a dark corner at the back of the guardhouse stood a small closet with a heavy wooden doorframe. Darrell could just see the outline of a flaming symbol as it began to glow a deep red on the wooden surface. Beside the glowing symbol was the charred remains of the image of an eight-armed candlestick. The friar's menorah.

Kate was already holding hands with Brodie and she smiled tremulously at Darrell. "Try not to let go of my hand this time," she whispered.

"I'll do my best." Darrell wound her fingers through Delaney's rope collar and, grasping Kate's hand firmly, followed her friends through the low doorway.

Chapter Six

Darrell handed around the last of the peppermints from her pocket as they sat on the stairs, recovering. Delaney lay on the bottom step, panting gently.

Brodie patted his head. "You're an amazing dog, you know that?" He looked up at the soot and dirt-stained girls. "He always seems so unperturbed by these journeys."

"I've never come back without my clothes ripped to shreds," said Kate, pointing at the dirty bare knee poking through her jeans, "and he always looks like he's just been to the groomers."

"So, what do you think happened to Paris?" asked Darrell.

"Well, he wasn't touching us when we went through the portal," said Brodie, "so he must still be here somewhere. He couldn't have travelled with us."

"He's probably gone back up to the school," said Kate. "We're going to need to talk to him to find out what he knows — he had to have seen us get pulled away."

"I thought he got dragged along for sure," said Darrell quietly. "Especially when the friar said he had found my three friends." Delaney flopped over on his side to let her rub his tummy. "I'm just so glad you're both okay," she said in a low voice. "I've been sick with worry. Where were you all that time?"

"We stayed at the little villa where we found you," said Brodie. "We looked everywhere for you when we arrived in Lisbon. Of course, it took us quite a while to figure out where we were at first. Kate was convinced we had to be in Spain because of what we had been learning in Professor Grampian's class."

"Well, that's how it worked before with Professor Tooth," Kate said, a trifle crankily.

"Anyway, we couldn't find you anywhere. We searched a bit through the passages near the guardhouse under the castle, but then Kate thought you must have gone out into the city, so we went out to look."

"I hit my head this time," said Darrell, ruefully rubbing the sore spot. "I must have been knocked out for quite a while. And I *was* in a passageway, near a little underground grotto."

"Anyway," continued Brodie, "we finally figured out we were in Lisbon. We asked around in the local marketplace to see if anyone had seen you."

"I pretended you were my lost sister," interjected Kate. "Nobody wanted to talk to us. Everyone seemed so anxious and suspicious because we were strangers."

"After what seemed like forever I spoke to a priest all hooded up in a red cloak who told us to go find Brother Socorro at the church — that he sometimes gave lost travellers sanctuary."

"A red robe?" said Darrell thoughtfully. "Why does that remind me of something?" She thought a moment then shook her head. "It's gone. So his name is Brother Socorro, eh?"

"Yeah. Turned out he was actually looking for us, since he must have found you by then."

"He hid me in his room in the cathedral," Darrell explained. "But he locked me in, and I guess that's when things started to go crazy in the city, so he left me there for what seemed like forever."

"Nearly three days," said Kate, patting Darrell on the arm.

"No wonder I was so hungry! So you were in the cottage all that time?" asked Darrell.

"Only about a day, 'cause we spent the first day figuring out where we were and the second looking for you," Kate replied.

Darrell leaned over and squeezed Kate by the shoulders. "That explains why Socorro thought you were my sister," she said and peered at Brodie through bloodshot eyes. "You know, I am so tired, at one point I thought he actually referred to you as Kate's 'good husband.'"

Kate and Brodie both started talking at once.

"It was the only ..."

"... not my idea ..."

"... a short time ..."

"And nobody has to know anything about it," they both blurted.

Darrell dropped her head onto her arms and enjoyed the best laugh she could remember having for a long time. When she finally looked up, she saw Kate's face was scarlet, and even Brodie's cheeks had reddened.

"There was no other way," he said, standing up abruptly. "There was no one else to act as chaperone, and in those days, no decent girl would be wandering around alone with a guy unless she was married to him."

Darrell's face was sore from grinning. "He was saving your reputation, Kate," she spluttered.

Kate rolled her eyes. "Grow up, will you? It was the only thing we could think of to explain ourselves to Brother Socorro."

Darrell chuckled. "Okay, okay, I'll try to keep it to myself."

Kate yawned hugely. "I am so ready for a nap," she said, rubbing her eyes. "A person can take only so much anxiety, you know." She stood up.

"What's that?" Darrell turned to peer down one of the passages. Delaney lifted his head and cocked one of his ears.

"There's a light." Kate looked like she was ready to run. "We'd better get out of here."

Brodie put his hand on Kate's arm. "Just a second."

The beam of light broadened, and from around the curve in the passage appeared Paris, his hair glowing the faintest lavender in the thin light.

"Thought so," muttered Brodie.

"Sheesh — you really know how to scare a guy," said Paris, his voice hoarse. "I've been searching down here for hours, yelling my fool head off."

Darrell laughed nervously. "I'm so sorry Paris." She swallowed. "We've been — we've been looking for you, too."

Kate sat back down with a shaky sigh. "How long have we been lost?" she asked.

Paris directed the beam onto his watch. "A little more than two hours," he said. He bent down and ruffled Delaney's fur. "I thought I'd be able to find you for sure, boy," he said and directed his flashlight upward. "What happened back there? Where did that wind come from? It was almost like it blew you all right out of here. By the time I got the dust out of my eyes I couldn't find you anywhere."

"Yeah," Darrell shot a significant glance at Kate. "We got separated, too. Just found each other a few minutes ago."

Kate nodded. "Yup. How 'bout that wind, anyway?" She lifted an eyebrow at Brodie. "You're the expert underground. Maybe you can tell us how a hurricane like that can blow through a tunnel this far from the edge of the ocean."

Brodie curled his lip at her, and Kate grinned.

"Beats me," he said, finally. "But I think we should get out of here before it happens again."

"Me too," said Paris, though he shot a strange glance at Darrell. Delaney trotted up the first few steps and then paused to wait for the rest of the group to follow. "Your dog sure seems comfortable down here," said Paris.

Darrell looked at him sharply, disturbed by the tone of his voice. "I don't know what you mean," she said lightly. "Delaney is always the same, happy to go for a walk anywhere."

"Really?" Paris echoed. He gestured for Brodie and Kate to pass, and when they did, he put his hand on Darrell's arm. "I think we need to talk," he said quietly.

Darrell looked carefully into his face in the dim

glow of the flashlight. "You might be right," she said with a sigh, then followed the group up the treacherous stone steps.

CHAPTER SEVEN

The flames were burning and someone was dragging her closer. She could feel the pull on her shoulder — smell the burning flesh. She opened her mouth to scream ...

"My goodness, dear. It's only a bad dream."

Darrell opened her eyes to the placid face of Mrs. Follett. She sat up in bed, befuddled. "Mrs. Follett? What are you doing here?"

"Well, it *is* eleven o'clock. I know it's a Sunday and you young folks need your rest, but I thought I should wake you as there is a call from your mother in the Middle East."

Darrell flipped over onto her stomach and reached under the bed for her prosthesis. Three days back from the journey to Inquisition-torn Lisbon and she still hadn't caught up on her sleep. "Thanks get me, Mrs. Follett. I'll be down

...orry dear, your mother told me she would
...n fifteen minutes, so you have time to get
...' Mrs. Follett bustled over to the window and
back the curtains. "Raining again today, I'm
...d," she said, and scurried out of the room.

Darrell looked around as she adjusted her prosthesis. Lily's bed was empty and neatly made, and Kate's
looked like a charging rhino had roared through it.
Darrell grinned at the glimpse of tousled red hair
sprouting like a patch of hawk weed from somewhere
near the bottom of the bed.

She pulled on her jeans and reached into the back
pocket to pull out a creased and torn piece of paper.
Folding the page carefully, she replaced it in her
pocket and shook her friend by the shoulder. "Wake
up, Katie. I'll meet you downstairs in the dining
hall, okay?"

No reply.

A moment later as Darrell was lacing up her shoes,
Lily came bounding into the room, bearing a load of
swimming paraphernalia.

"You mean she's not up yet?" sniffed Lily, disdainfully. "I've been up since six, swimming laps."

Darrell grinned. "If anyone can wake her up, Lily,
you can. Go for it." She left the room to the sound of

a torrent of abuse erupting from somewhere under Kate's bedclothes.

"I don't know what to tell Paris," Darrell said. It was late in the afternoon, and after a reassuring talk with her mother, she had managed to drag Kate out from under the covers. Brodie sat beside Kate, the waning light of a grey afternoon casting sepia shadows in the empty study hall. Darrell's mother was deeply involved in a peacekeeping effort but still managing to stay out of the hot zone, and Darrell was relieved to hear her sounding so happy. Less comforting was how often her mother referred to Dr. Asa. By the end of the conversation, Darrell was convinced that almost every sentence she'd heard had been prefaced with "David and I." Still, it was reassuring to know that there was someone watching her mother's back — *as long as he keeps his mind on his job,* she thought. It meant Darrell could turn her attention to a more immediate concern, in the form of one Paris Mercer — the troublemaker.

"Don't tell him anything," snapped Kate, still not quite recovered from Lily's rude awakening technique. "All he needs to know is that we all got lost down there, it's not a safe place to go, and that's that."

"I did tell him that," said Darrell, "but he just looks at me like he doesn't believe me."

"I'm with Kate," said Brodie. "I think if you keep changing the subject, he'll drop it sooner or later."

"Okay, I guess." Darrell fiddled with the folded page she had pulled from her pocket. "I've got something to read to you," she blurted. "I've been going over it, and I think it can mean only one thing."

She quickly related story of examining the old ledgers in the cottage while waiting for Brother Socorro to return. "He obviously felt they were really important or he wouldn't have tried to hide them from the soldiers," she said. "I think they must have held a list of initials of the people he had helped save from the Inquisition in Spain."

"He didn't tell us anything about his life when we were with him." said Brodie, "He did say that many *conversos* had escaped to Portugal, but that it was no longer safe. I think he believed we were all trying to do just that."

"*Conversos?*" Darrell repeated the word slowly, and her fingers traced across the worn paper on the table in front of her.

"*Conversos* were the Jews that were persecuted by the Inquisition for their religion," said Brodie. "Remember what Gramps told us?" He whipped open his notebook and read: "Queen Isabella of Castile, a devout Catholic, was also a bold warrior. She and her husband, Ferdinand of Aragon, had united Spain and were seeking to strengthen their territory against the Spanish Moors. One way to get the money for this expensive war was to take it from their own countrymen. The money was raised when Isabella declared her personal confessor the head of the Inquisition and gave him the right to torture and murder anyone not a member of the Roman Catholic Church as a way to convince them to change their minds." He closed his notebook.

Kate nodded. "And if the people agreed to convert, their souls were deemed saved, but they were still put to death and their money confiscated for the war effort," she added.

"But the soldiers who chased us called us *marranos*," said Darrell. "Not *conversos*."

"The people who converted were often called pigs," said Kate sadly. "We heard that expression everywhere on the streets of Lisbon. It seems some people didn't believe that the *conversos* had truly accepted Christianity."

"It also made it easier to kill them," said Brodie, flatly. "It's easier to slaughter pigs than kill your fellow human beings, I guess."

"So Socorro thought he was saving us from the Inquisition," said Darrell, quietly, "when really he was leading us to an old friend."

"An old friend?" Kate looked surprised. "What are you talking about?"

Darrell unfolded her piece of paper and smoothed it out on the table. The page looked incredibly old and worn, its creases brittle to the point of breaking.

"Where did that come from?" asked Kate.

"I brought it back with me," said Darrell eagerly. "I copied it out from the back of one of Socorro's ledgers. Listen:

> March 17, 1505
> Numbers slowing down, the wealthy are more able to pay for passage abroad. Have taken on an assistant, a young man from one of the madhouses of Madrid where I went to offer what little help I could. The wars and rule of Torquemada brought much pain to so many and this boy has suffered beyond any I had seen. Still, he has been a great help thus far and I plan to further train him in the earthly goal of kindness to all things that is so sorely missing from these times.

"Then he goes on a bit about how perhaps it is the people that the church calls insane are really the only ones thinking straight, so I skipped that bit, but listen to this ...

June 11, 1505

My new assistant has proved to be of enormous help in redirecting the conversos. He raves less often about what he calls his "old life" but has much to say of his experiences getting caught up in war and mayhem on his way from Florence to Madrid. He has surely been sent by God himself to help me with the plight of these poor people.

Darrell looked up at Kate and Brodie. "Do you see? He spoke to me about an assistant, too. And I think it must be Conrad!"

Kate shook her head. "I think it should be you in the madhouse, Darrell. How can you make a connection like that? What makes you think it was Conrad? It could have been anyone."

"Look, I didn't have time to copy out any of the part with the messy handwriting, but I feel sure it was notes taken by Conrad. Kate, I think he was there all along. It was 1506, right? That is only three years past the time when we left him behind in the fire. Don't you see? He could still be alive!"

The study door closed softly behind them.

Brodie looked over his shoulder nervously. "Better keep your voice down, Darrell," he said quietly. "You may be right, though it sounds more like a coincidence to me."

"It's no coincidence," said Darrell. "You guys, I need to go back there. There has to be some meaning to these trips into time — otherwise why would this evidence just become available under our noses? It can't just be coincidence."

Kate jumped to her feet. "Look, Darrell, these notes could be about anybody. If it is Conrad, how did he end up in a madhouse in Madrid? He stayed behind in Florence. Italy is a long way from Spain."

"It said in the notes that he had come from Florence!" Darrell slammed her hand on the table. "It's him, I know it."

"Okay, calm down, calm down," said Brodie. "We can't do anything about it right now, anyway. And keep your voice down, Darrell, or we'll be explaining our-selves to the whole school, next." He pulled out a blank sheet of paper. "How does this sound? We have to do research for Gramps's project anyway, so let's find out more."

He started making notes. "We need to find out all we can about the Inquisition and also about the Protestant Reformation that followed it. Everything was changing in Europe at the time, maybe we can find the key to what was really going on."

"Look — this isn't going to get us any closer to

finding out if Conrad survived the fire," said Darrell impatiently. "I vote we just go back and take our chances. The portals through time have never steered us wrong before."

"Are you kidding? You can't just go back into that crazy time without knowing a bit more about it," said Kate, her voice rising. "We got out of there just as two thousand people were about to be massacred in one day. In *one day*, Darrell! There's no way I'm going back unless I know that we will be as safe as possible when we arrive, especially to find someone as unpleasant as Conrad."

"Listen, you two." Brodie pointed to his notes, his voice calm. "If Darrell researches everything she can find about the Spanish Inquisition, I'll do the Portuguese, and Kate, you can look into the Reformation. It'll help with our projects for Gramps and it will help us be more informed about what we're getting ourselves into if we decide to go back."

"*When* we decide to go back, you mean," said Darrell pointedly.

"Okay, whatever you say, Darrell. I just don't think we have enough information to make any decision yet."

Darrell stood up. "We meet in one week," she said quietly. "Then, information or not, I'm going back to try to find Conrad. Come on, Delaney." She picked up her books and headed for the library, without a backward glance at the worried looks on the faces of her two best friends.

The rain continued to fall, and Eagle Glen School sat wet and shrouded in fog on its viewpoint high above the water. Darrell glanced at her watch as she sat in the late afternoon light of the school art room. She was putting the finishing touches on a streetscape in watercolours. At the bottom of the painting coursed the Rio Tejo and lining its banks were the crowded homes in the vivid Portuguese colours that she remembered from her quick climb through the hilly landscape of Lisbon. At the top right corner she had just sketched in the outline of the magnificent Castelo de São Jorge, St. George's Castle. It was hard not to think of it as "the fortress," Brother Socorro's name for the place.

"Time to wrap things up, don't you think?" Mr. Gill was washing brushes in the large sink.

"Uh — I guess so." It always took Darrell a few minutes to come back into the real world after working on one of her paintings. She dragged herself out of sixteenth-century Portugal and smiled at her art teacher.

"That's what I like to see," he said heartily, "an artist who enjoys her work."

Darrell joined Mr. Gill at the sink and started to wash the paint off her hands. He was right — she did enjoy her work. She enjoyed it not only for the creativity it allowed her to channel onto the canvas but also for the break it gave her from the worries that haunted the rest of her life. She'd spent the last week studying everything she could find about the Inquisition. It was a terrible time and set the stage for much of the change that was to sweep through Europe in the subsequent centuries.

And yet … *If I know about all the most dreadful events and I deliberately stay out of the way, why can't I go back and find one person — one small, insignificant person — a person who doesn't belong there anyway? Why can't I find him and bring him home?*

She finished cleaning up and waved an absent goodbye to Mr. Gill. Delaney padded after her, a purple daub on one furry ear, as she hurried down the hall to meet her friends.

Brodie looked over at Darrell's pile of books and grinned. He pulled a slim file folder out of his backpack. "It's all here," he said, flipping open the file.

"I don't think so." Kate raised a skeptical eyebrow. "I've managed to open fourteen separate computer files just on Martin Luther alone. How did you condense the whole of the Spanish Inquisition down into a single file?"

"Not only a single file," Brodie said smugly, "but a single page. It's all in the note taking, Kate. Really, you should pay more attention in class — it would save you so much time."

He held up his folder just in time to deflect the eraser Kate threw at him. "And it's good for defensive manoeuvres as well," he said, his eyes twinkling at Darrell.

"Quit teasing her and tell us what you've got," pleaded Darrell. "Every day we dawdle around here at Eagle Glen means finding Conrad is going to be that much harder."

Kate stopped throwing things. "We are never going to find him, Darrell. You have to just get used to the idea that Conrad is gone for good."

"For good? What's good about it? I feel like I condemned the guy to some kind of hell on earth."

Brodie sighed. "Darrell, we've been through this before. What happened to Conrad was not your fault. It was his poor decision-making combined with simple bad luck. You had nothing to do with it."

"I know, I know. I just wish I could talk things out with Professor Tooth."

"Now that *is* weird, come to think of it. She's still not back," mused Brodie. "I've gotten kinda used to Gramps."

"I've gotten used to Paris tormenting Gramps,"

said Kate. "The sorry thing is that the old fellow doesn't even seem to notice."

"I'm going to notice when I get Paris's mark on my report card and he gets mine," said Brodie glumly. "Gramps still hasn't figured out who I am."

Darrell tapped Brodie's file folder with her charcoal pencil. "Can we get on with this, please? Tell us what you've got."

"Okay, here goes." He cleared his throat. "There was a lot of messing around between the kings and queens and the church, basically a big power struggle that lasted for generations. In the end, royalty decided that they were answerable only to God — it was called the 'Divine Right of Kings.' So if you were a king or a queen, you got to make all the rules. As you can imagine, this didn't sit well with the common folk. But it was like we saw in the Middle Ages and the Renaissance: religion was still a big part of everybody's life — even royalty. They all believed that God was on their side."

Darrell nodded. "Remember how often the people prayed during the time of the Black Plague? They were in church two or three times a day."

"Okay, but that was just Europe, right?" said Kate. "What about everywhere else? Not everyone was a Christian."

"No kidding," said Brodie. "Try half the world. And, not surprisingly, that was the source of a lot of strife.

KC DYER

Almost right from the start, European Christians were running off on crusades, trying to convert the heathen."

"Except the people the Christians called heretics and barbarians were not always ready to agree to convert so easily," said Kate.

"And that's what happened in Spain," continued Brodie. "When Ferdinand of Aragon married Isabella of Castile it was a big deal, because the two of them were both heir to huge kingdoms. Their marriage basically solidified Spain into a country for the first time. Since they were both strong Catholics they decided to make it the religion of all the people."

"Is this where the torturing comes in?" said Kate, shuddering.

"Sort of," admitted Brodie. "Isabella had her own personal priest, and she appointed him head Inquisitor. The Catholic Church had been supporting the conversion of Jews, Muslims, and people of other faiths for centuries. Isabella just gave her priest the right to speed up the process in Spain. His name was Tomás de Torquemada."

Darrell dropped her pencil with a clatter. "Brother Socorro mentioned him," she said quickly. "He said something about Torquemada being a quick route to the flames."

Brodie nodded. "Yeah, well, that was his preferred method of conversion. If someone was accused of practising another religion — usually Judaism — in secret, they were sentenced to be burned at the stake. However, they were given a chance to be baptized as a Christian before being burned. If they chose to convert to Christianity, their sentence was commuted."

"So they would live?" asked Kate.

"Nope. They got their heads cut off first, though. Considered a much more merciful death."

Darrell winced. "Quicker, anyway."

"No kidding. And the people who refused to kiss the cross were burned to death at a stake surrounded with green wood, so that it took longer to consume them in flames."

Kate put her hands over her ears. Her skin had gone stark white. "And this is where you want to go traipsing back to find Conrad?" she whispered. "You think that he would have survived in such a barbaric time?"

"Oh, but you've got that wrong, Kate," said Brodie. "The Christians did not see themselves as barbarians. They were purifying everyone else's barbarian souls through fire." He turned over his page. "It didn't hurt that the Spanish needed money to finance the wars against the Moors, either. So in 1492, ten years after he had taken over as head Inquisitor, Torquemada introduced the great expulsion."

"I know about that," interrupted Darrell. She pulled out the book her uncle had given her for her birthday. "This is just a novel, but it tells a lot about a family who escaped from Spain during the expulsion," she said, and flipped through the dog-eared pages. "Like, here's a section where they talk about climbing through the mountains to Portugal …"

Kate snorted. "And a lot of good that did them," she said. "The king of Portugal started his own Inquisition just a few years later."

"It's weird," said Darrell slowly. "Everyone seemed to think that theirs was the only way to heaven. The Islamic Moors fought the Christians and the Christians slaughtered the Jews."

"Kinda like watching the eleven o'clock news today," said Brodie gloomily. "I never know who the dead bodies belong to, but they almost always belong to one religious faction or another."

"Okay, you guys, we're getting off track here," said Darrell impatiently. "Kate, what did you find out about Martin Luther?"

Kate flipped open the lid of her laptop and tapped a few buttons. "Well, like I said, there's a lot of stuff out there about him. But it all comes down to this. He was a priest in Germany and he got pretty fed up with the Catholic Church, primarily for selling indulgences, which were kind of a get-out-of-jail-free card for the rich. According to what I read, they could pay the church for an indulgence, which would guarantee them or a member of their family a place in heaven."

Brodie laughed. "Hey, I'd like one of those!"

Kate grinned. "Anyway, he wrote down all his complaints — ninety-five of them — and nailed them onto the door of a church. This was pretty much the start of the Reformation movement in Germany."

"So after all the violence of the Spanish Inquisition and with a lot of corruption everywhere in the Catholic Church, people started protesting against the church all over Europe," said Brodie. "In France, the protestors were called the Huguenots."

"And in Scotland, a guy called John Knox started protests, too."

Darrell flipped open one of her books. "But that wasn't until the middle of the sixteenth century," she said impatiently. "That's too late. We need to figure out where Conrad is based on what we know about things at the beginning of the Reformation. Here's what we know." She began counting off items on her fingers. "One: Socorro was helping people escape from the Inquisition, right? Mostly Jewish people, but probably a few others as well. Two: he had a helper of some sort whose name he wouldn't tell us. And," she waved three fingers in the air, "I found that book, which looked like a ledger, but with long lists of letters. I *think* they were initials of the people that Socorro helped. And in the back of that book was a diary — and I am sure part of it was written by Conrad."

"Okay, Darrell, if you're making lists, here's one for you," said Kate. "One: Conrad hated school and hated writing. He's the last person in the world who would keep a diary. Two: even if it was Conrad's diary, the last we saw of Socorro was as he was being taken away by guards. He probably didn't survive the night. And three: finding a person lost in time is harder than finding a needle in a haystack." She sat back in her chair. "We should just leave well enough alone."

Darrell jumped up. "You're wrong, Kate," she said furiously. "But you are welcome to stay here. There is a reason that portal took us back to the Portuguese Inquisition. I believe the reason was for us to meet Brother Socorro. And at the bottom of those steps in the secret passage there is a tunnel full of portals. If I have to explore all of them to find out what happened to Conrad, I will."

Brodie reached out and pulled Darrell back down into her chair. "Just calm down for a minute, willya?" he said quietly. "How much of this is really about Conrad, Darrell?"

She turned on him furiously. "Now what does *that* mean?"

Brodie shared an uneasy glance with Kate. "It means — uh — well, it means that you lost your dad when you were really young, and in a horrible way." His words came tumbling out before she could object.

"You lost your dad and you lost your foot, and I think you put Conrad into the same category and you feel like you've lost him, too. But the truth of the matter is," Brodie stopped and took a deep breath, "the truth is that none of these things are your fault, Darrell. You have to quit trying to fix things and quit blaming yourself. Maybe you just need to let it all go."

Darrell felt ready to explode. She opened her mouth to roar at Brodie, but suddenly closed it instead. She dropped her face into her hands and stayed that way for several long moments. When she sat up again, her face was calm.

"Maybe you're right, Brodie. I've had a pretty crazy life so far. Maybe I just need to let things look after themselves for a while."

Kate's jaw dropped and she let out a whoop. "I don't believe it. Way to go, Brodie! I never thought you'd get her to see the light!" She turned to Darrell and hugged her. "This is the right decision, Darrell. You need to spend some time worrying about your art and your school work. Just be a normal kid for a while."

Darrell nodded. "Yeah. And my Uncle Frank offered to take me shopping in Vancouver over the weekend, so maybe I'll take him up on it. Just give myself a break."

"Nobody deserves it more," beamed Kate.

CHAPTER EIGHT

A tinny beeping sound in her ear woke Darrell, and she sat up, feeling groggy and disoriented. How had she fallen asleep? She'd been so worried she thought it would be no trouble to stay awake. So much for taking a break. She'd take a break when she'd managed to find Conrad and bring him back to Eagle Glen where he belonged.

She reached down and felt around beside her bed for her prosthesis. Everything else she needed was bundled into a spare pillowcase on her bed. She adjusted her leg and then piled the bedclothes into a lump that she hoped would resemble a sleeping figure. It wouldn't matter anyway — she'd covered any questions by giving everyone the line about Uncle Frank taking her shopping. Everyone knew he was an early riser. She'd just say she left before anyone woke up. That gave her two full days to find Conrad, which meant a lot of time in the strangely condensed world of the past. More time than she'd ever need.

An almost full moon shone through the curved glass of the window, with Venus gleaming brightly beneath and both reflected back on the countless waves below. Delaney's tail thumped once on the floor, but Darrell had remembered to bring up a few biscuits to bribe him into silence. It was a happy dog, licking his chops, that followed the shadow of a girl down the quiet school hallway towards the library door.

The school was old and full of its own noises in this first hour of a February morning. It creaked and shivered like an old man dreaming, and Darrell jumped and hid in a doorway more than once, only to find it was just the old building, settling in its sleep. She closed the library door behind Delaney with a sigh of relief. All abed and none the wiser — just the way she wanted it.

"I think we'll just skip the lights, okay boy?" she whispered to Delaney. "Don't want to attract attention now that we're in the clear."

Delaney dashed to the back of the long room ahead of Darrell, and she made her way more cautiously along one of the lengthy corridors, running her fingers along the spines of the books to guide herself through the dark. She could hear Delaney snuffling happily near the hidden entranceway, and she reached into her cloth bag for a small flashlight. When a light shone into her face and blinded her, she continued to muddle around in the bag for a moment, thinking she had somehow switched it on.

"What a relief. One more night on this floor and I would have probably given up and gone back to my bed for good."

The sound of the voice nearly sent her through the roof. She squeaked and dropped her bag, scattering the items at her feet.

"Geez, Darrell, I didn't know you were so easy to scare."

Darrell was beyond furious. "Paris! What are you doing here? And would you get that light out of my face, please?" She sank to her knees and found her own flashlight, switching it on before loading her other dropped possessions back into her bag.

"So, you want the long story or the short one?"

Darrell stared at him in exasperation. "The short one," she hissed.

Paris nodded knowingly. "Ah yes, places to go, things to do, eh, Darrell?"

"What do you know about what I have to do?" she shot back.

"I know more than you think I do, anyway," he said quietly. "It's amazing what a person can pick up around this school if you just listen carefully."

Darrell couldn't believe it. "Have you been listening to my conversations?"

Paris shrugged and began rolling up his sleeping bag.

"Just what do you think you're doing?" she whispered furiously.

"Going with you," he said simply.

"No — not a chance — no way. There's no hope of that, so you might as well just pack up now and go back to bed."

"He was my friend too, y'know."

Darrell was stunned. "How much *do* you know?" she asked slowly.

Paris stood up and leaned his lanky frame against the bookcase. "I know you're looking for Conrad," he said, keeping his voice low. "And you may think that I'm stupid, Darrell, but I know that when I lost you guys down in the secret passageway that you were not there the whole time. I searched every accessible corridor and you were all gone — including Delaney." He reached down to pat the dog. "No way you were just lost down there. I've been down twice since then to double-check. You were *gone*, Darrell, I know that for sure. And when I heard you talking last week in the study hall, I figured you might do something about it soon. Now the time has come to tell me all about it. Maybe I can actually be a help."

Darrell shook her head, mentally kicking herself for not stopping to find out who had been eavesdropping in study hall that afternoon. "I can't tell you about it and I can't take you, Paris. You just don't understand. I can't afford to lose you, too."

"Lose me? You *lost* Conrad? I don't think so, Darrell. I know there's more to this than you're telling me."

Darrell thought fast. After a moment she nodded. "You're right, Paris. Okay, you win — I will tell you. But you know I can't tell you without Brodie and Kate. They are a part of this too. You go get them, and I'll tell you the whole story."

"I have to wake Kate up in the middle of the night? Not a chance," he said, shaking his head. "Brodie's at least got a bit of a sense of humour — but Kate? No way."

Darrell crossed her arms. "Well, that's the deal. If you want to know more, go get 'em and we'll tell you together. Otherwise the deal's off."

Paris thought for a long moment. "All right," he said at last. "But be patient — this might take me a few minutes."

Darrell nodded. "Just don't wake Lily, whatever you do," she warned. "I'll never hear the end of it if she misses some of her beauty sleep because of me."

She sat down beside Delaney and ran her fingers through the thick hair under his collar as Paris strode off. "Get ready to run, dog," she whispered. "Our window of opportunity just got a whole lot smaller."

"Twenty-eight, twenty-nine, thirty. Okay, boy, let's go." Darrell didn't have the patience to count to fifty, but she figured that thirty was enough to get Paris out of the library and down the hall to the boys' rooms. Paris would be smart enough to get Brodie up first in order to get his help in awakening Kate.

She had yanked open the heavy bookcase and shone her flashlight into the dark cavern beyond when she came upon the first snag.

"I'm going to need to close this door, Delaney," she whispered. "That stupid Paris has really messed things up for me." The closed door would at least slow the group down when they came to find her, and by the time they reached the bottom, she and Delaney would have gone through the portal and they would be out of luck.

"That's the beauty of this little gig," she said to Delaney after the heavy door swung closed behind them and they had started down the stairs. "Anybody can have a dog who fetches sticks or rolls over. It takes someone pretty special to have a time-travelling dog." She grinned at the sight of his tail, wagging on each step as he spiralled down the tightly winding stair.

At the bottom, Darrell paused to set down the pillowcase. She didn't want to risk carrying the whole bag. She had carried things both backwards and forwards through time before, but the results could be a bit unpredictable. Wristwatches, for example, disappeared completely, and things like pencils would often take an entirely different form. The most important thing to remember was her roll of peppermints, and she tucked that carefully in her pocket with a number of other essentials that she hoped would safely make the trip.

At last she was ready. "It's decision time, Delaney," she whispered. Which doorway would it be?

A sound from the stairs made her head snap up. It couldn't be! There was no way Paris had had time to wake Brodie and Kate and get back to the library, but she didn't dare wait to find out. Grabbing Delaney by the collar she stepped forward toward one of the doorways to the right. A symbol in the shape of a falcon began to glow hot and red on the frame of the door and she smelled the unmistakeable scent of burning wood. The smell caused her to hesitate for one fatal second, and as she stepped forward a flying figure leapt from the stairs and tackled her right through the doorway.

"You idiot!" She was so angry she just wanted to kick him, but at the last minute she redirected her foot into a nearby wall. "Ow!"

"Oh, man," Paris rolled on the ground, his face ashen. "Oh, man. Don't look Darrell, I'm going to be …"

And sick he was, all over himself and the floor and even the wall beside him. Darrell rolled herself out of the way and got wearily to her feet. She popped a peppermint from her pocket into her mouth and looked around the room. They were in a small cottage, very similar to the one in Lisbon, with a major difference. This one smelled beautiful. Well — it had until Paris had christened it. The windows were thrown open to catch a fresh spring breeze, and Darrell could see that they were somewhere in a deep forest. Not a city in sight.

But first things first. She rolled up the sleeves of her dress and helped Paris to a small stool that sat near the fireplace.

"Here, put this in your mouth. It'll make you feel better. I'll clean up the mess."

Paris hung his head in misery, sucking on his peppermint. "I'm sorry, Darrell," he said humbly. "I just couldn't let you go without me." He tried to lift his head and winced at the effort. His eyes widened until Darrell worried they would fall out of the sockets. He didn't say another word as she swept up the mess that he'd made of the rushes on the floor and deposited the whole sorry pile outside.

At last he got to his feet and staggered up. "Just a minute," he said in a strangled voice, and dashed off into the bushes. Darrell could hear him being sick again.

"Serves him right, the creep," she muttered to herself as she replaced the twig broom in the corner where she'd found it. "He's just going to slow me down, and now I have to explain everything to him *and* look after him. Ugh!"

After a few moments, Paris returned, still shamefaced. "I don't know what's making me sick like this," he said apologetically. "Maybe if I just sit down for a few minutes it will pass."

"It's time sickness," she said flatly. "And it usually passes faster if you eat a couple of mints right away. Something in the sugar and the peppermint settles your stomach somehow."

"Geez, it didn't seem to work that way for me, but I'll try it again," he said and looked around slowly. "Time sickness. As in — travelling through time?" As she passed him another mint he stared unabashedly at her dress.

"You look beautiful, Darrell, but can you please tell me what's going on here? Why are you in that long dress with your hair all done up like that?" He gestured out the door where Delaney lay curled in the sun. "And what's with the dog?"

Darrell rolled her eyes. "What's going on here is that you are causing me nothing but trouble. It's going to take forever to explain all this to you, and I have more important things to do than to baby you along while I find Conrad."

An odd look crossed Paris's face, and he dashed for the door, retching. He returned moments later, wiping his mouth.

"Why don't you just give me the short version, Darrell? And by the way, I don't buy your peppermint theory. It's not working for me at all."

Half an hour and only two vomiting sessions later, Darrell had Paris briefed and ready to head out on a reconnaissance mission. His head was spinning with the novelty of all he saw about him. "These are the coolest clothes," he said, running his hands down the heavy linen shirt and wool trousers. "The underwear is a little itchy, though." He was grinning broadly in spite of his uncertain digestive condition.

Darrell had to smile. "The itchiness helps you realize it's not just a weird dream or hallucination," she said quietly. "And I have to say, you're taking it better than I did on my first journey. I was scared to death."

"Darrell, this is the most awesome thing that has ever happened to me — apart from the barfing part, I mean." He grabbed Darrell's hand as they walked out the door. "Thank you so much for taking the time to explain everything to me. I can't believe it — this is just amazing."

He paused to watch the awkward hop-skip step that Darrell had to use to walk on the antique wooden foot that her prosthesis had morphed into over the course of the journey.

"How do you walk on that thing?"

She shrugged. "I manage. It's easier if I have a cane of some sort, but if I can hold onto your arm, we'll get along okay."

"Uh — all right — just a minute." He dashed off into the bushes. Darrell crossed her arms impatiently, but he emerged in seconds, looking a little pale. "Sorry. Not much left in there now, so it's not taking as long, at least."

She sighed loudly and marched on.

He lifted his chin defiantly and ran to take her arm again. "Look, I know you're mad at me. But I promise to make it up to you. I've spent a lot of time in woodworking class over the years, and I'm going to carve you the nicest walking stick you've ever seen, just to make up for all the trouble I've caused."

"Forget it," said Darrell flatly. "We're just not going to have time. We've got to figure out where we are first and then find out where to locate Brother Socorro. And even if we manage all that, we still have to find Conrad, if Socorro will lead us to him." She softened her tone a little. "You're going to have to be my walking stick for now, okay? Besides, if I keep my hands on you, maybe you won't be able to mess things up any more than you already have."

They crossed to the edge of the small clearing in the trees.

"Which way do we go now?" asked Paris.

"That depends," said a lilting voice behind them, "on where you would most like to find yourself."

"So tell me anew how you came to be here?" The young woman's dark eyes sparkled at Paris.

"We — uh — we travelled through the woods, and—"

"And we'd come here because we were told we could find a Franciscan priest," interrupted Darrell. "His name is Brother Socorro and ..."

The young woman gasped. She looked around carefully, and when she spoke, her voice had lost its lightness. "I know of the dear brother," she said quietly. "And though we are fairly safe here, the trees are filled with hunters and the castle is very nearby." She looked at them critically. "Let us go inside the cottage and I will tell you all I know."

Paris jumped up. "I'll — I'll be right there," he said quickly and fled into the bushes.

The young woman raised her eyebrows.

Darrell shook her head. "Bad stomach," she said with a little grin. "Must have been something he ate."

The young woman waited at the door and allowed Darrell to hold it open for her before sweeping inside.

Darrell took the initiative right away. "My name is Dara," she said quickly. "And the fellow being sick outside is my — my brother, Paris."

The young woman smiled and her face lit up like a beacon. "*Une de mes villes favori*," she said merrily. "One of my favourite cities. And yet I have never heard of anyone named for the place, except the famous Paris from Greek mythology, of course."

"I'm afraid we have become a little lost," Darrell said quickly. "Can you tell me exactly where we are?"

"Of course I can," came the pert reply. "You are in the gamekeeper's cottage in the forest of Windsor, and fortunately enough for you, it's haunted."

Paris returned after a few moments away and managed to keep his stomach settled for the duration of the young woman's visit. She identified herself as Nan Bullen, a lady-in-waiting to Queen Katherine, wife of King Henry VIII.

"Henry the Eighth," said Paris. He glanced at Darrell in astonishment. "What have we gotten ourselves into?"

Darrell widened her eyes at him, and he fell silent. Nan watched the exchange with interest, all the while adjusting her heavily ruffled black gloves. She looked over at Paris expectantly. "Do you feel better? You must tell me all you can of Brother Socorro."

"He has helped friends of mine in the past," said Darrell, not sure how much to give away. "The man I am truly looking for may have worked as an assistant to Brother Socorro." She took a deep breath and decided to risk all. "He helped *conversos* escape during the Spanish Inquisition," she said in a rush.

Nan ducked her head out the window and then carefully pulled the shutters closed. "It took long years for Socorro to escape the Inquisition," she said quietly. "He was in the clutches of the Inquisitors themselves for many months. But after his escape to England his interests broadened, and since we met, I have found his line of thinking to be very similar to my own."

She gestured around the room. "It was convenient for Socorro to use this cottage to help those who needed to leave the area because of persecution. A few well-placed rumours of hauntings kept the local villagers at bay, and since then this has been a safe place to help those in need."

She stood up and reached for a small, cloth-wrapped package she had set on the table earlier. "I'm afraid it is not much, but you are most welcome to it," she began. "The friar had not warned me of your coming, but I often carry a little something just in case."

Paris waved his hand, declining the offer. But Darrell was starving, so she helped herself to the food in Nan's bundle while the young woman continued chatting.

After the arduous journey and the work cleaning up after Paris, the grainy roll of bread, piece of hard cheese, and tiny, wrinkled apple tasted like a feast.

While Darrell ate, Nan stuck her head out of the shuttered window again. "Still no one about, thank the lord. What are your plans now that you are here?" she asked.

Darrell chewed a mouthful of apple.

"I am not sure," she said, choosing her words carefully. "I would most like to find Brother Socorro."

Nan shook her head. "I'm afraid that will not be possible. My apologies — I should have told you earlier. Brother Socorro is dead."

"Dead?" The taste of the apple turned bitter in Darrell's mouth. "How?"

"He was taken and killed by members of his own order in France. After the Lisbon Massacre, he was forced to take the escape route through which he had directed so many other souls, and he fled first to Turkey and then here to England. But he persisted in returning to France, and it was there he was exposed as an abettor of heretics. He was put to death by the sword." She dropped her head for a moment.

Darrell felt stunned. "I am so sorry," she whispered. "He was a good man."

"He was a saint," said Nan. "But his work carries on. I myself am very interested in the writings of Luther."

Nan looked at Darrell quizzically. "As a friend to Socorro, you are a follower of the words of Luther, are you not?"

"I have read of him," Darrell answered cautiously.

"So have I," said Paris from his darkened corner. Darrell jumped a little, having forgotten he was there. "He wrote ninety-five theses of complaint against his own church and was sanctioned for it by the pope," he said.

Darrell grinned. "You've been paying attention."

Paris nodded. "I have good teachers," he said quietly.

Darrell smiled a little. *Chalk one up for Gramps.*

Nan turned back to Darrell. "Now that you know Socorro has passed on, you must keep your thoughts of Luther and his ideas to yourselves," she said. "There are those that would have you treated as Socorro was, though I sense the times may well be changing."

She stood up. "My suggestion is that you find work at the castle. There has just been a terrible bout of sweating sickness through the town, and many of the servants are still ill and are unable to work."

She cast a critical eye over Paris. "As soon as your brother is feeling better, come up to the castle. I will see that work is found for you there. And together with the new friar, we can have many talks about the works and ideas of Luther."

"Thank you so much for your help, Nan," said Darrell gratefully. "Let me walk you out. Just a moment …"

She sat on a low stool and bent to adjust the material that bound the wooden foot and ankle to her leg. Glancing up, she was surprised that Nan did not turn away in disgust but stepped nearer to watch the process with interest.

"You were born this way?" she asked, adjusting the glove on her right hand as she spoke.

Darrell quickly resettled the cotton padding between her leg and the wooden casing. "No, I had an accident," she said, concentrating on rewrapping the cloth as tightly as she could. "I — uh," she looked up again and saw Nan's face, burning with a strange curiosity. "I fell off a horse and broke my ankle badly. It would not heal, and so the surgeon removed it."

"You are lucky to be alive," Nan said abruptly, tucking her hands under her arms. "With the drunken butcher that passes for a surgeon here, you would never have lived."

Darrell stood up. "Thank you again for helping us."

Nan waved away her thanks. Her black eyes sparkled in the candlelight. "This cottage will be a safe place for you to stay until we get you settled at court," she said. "The truth is, life with Katherine is so dull, conversing with Brother Socorro brought me a little excitement and certainly some knowledge I could get from no other source." She grinned, showing perfectly shaped white teeth. "I have missed it since he is gone, though Friar

Priamos looks like he will take over now that his mentor has gone. And besides ..." Her eyes twinkled merrily. "I have caught the eye of a new beau, a *very* powerful man. Who knows what will happen at court?"

CHAPTER NINE

The walk through to the village the next morning brought many memories back to Darrell, and she spent the time filling Paris in on some of the finer points of not giving either of them away.

"Just use the language as it comes naturally to you," she said with exasperation after he spent too long searching for a word when trying to tell her a story. "The slang we use every day isn't in this variety of English."

"I'm just not used to speaking Old English," complained Paris. "I keep trying to find the words to say what I mean and I can't."

"Believe it or not, this isn't Old English. It's modern English — the same English that Shakespeare will write in less than a hundred years."

"Shakespeare is considered modern? That's a good one. I can hardly manage 'to be or not to be.'"

"Paris, trust me, you'll be able to do it if you just relax and let it happen. How do you think I felt last year when I landed in fourteenth-century Scotland and found myself speaking Highland Gaelic?" She grinned. "Don't worry, you'll figure it out. And the sooner you relax, the sooner you'll stop feeling so sick."

For Paris was still showing signs of time sickness, though his vomiting had slowed to once every two or three hours. "I'll be fine," he assured Darrell after being sick immediately upon waking in the morning.

"I don't care about it, really," he said as they walked into town. "It's worth it to get to see this amazing time. I'll just make sure no one knows why I'm sick."

"Oh, yeah, they'd really understand that," said Darrell, snickering. "I'm sorry m'lady, I'm just puking in your petunias as a result of some kind of negative inter-action within the time-space continuum. Don't worry about a thing." She paused, feeling more serious. "The big worry is if they think you have the sweats or whatev-er they call dysentery in this century. They won't hire us if they think you are sick."

"I'll keep it under wraps," Paris promised through clenched teeth.

They entered the village and were immediately the subject of curious stares from the locals. Looking at the tiny thatched cottages reminded Darrell of the visits to Mallaig that seemed so long ago. The sight of the village square almost made her feel at home. Almost.

Darrell dropped her voice as she continued to tell Paris about what he might expect at the castle. "Just be polite and do what they tell you," she said. "I really need to talk with Nan about the friar she mentioned. I have the feeling he used to know Socorro. Maybe he can lead us to Conrad."

Paris started to look a little green again. "What is that smell?" he choked.

"I guess the sewage technology hasn't exactly advanced since my last trip," she muttered, fishing a lace handkerchief out of her pocket as they walked the high street up to the castle. Delaney capered at her heel, ears forward and eyes bright, doggishly enjoying the walk and all the smells that went with it.

Paris nodded. "Don't tell me that I'm seeing what I think I'm seeing running down this gutter." He stuffed his own handkerchief over his mouth and nose.

"Yep," said Darrell. "But it could be worse. In Scotland the women would call out 'gardy-loo' and then throw the contents of their chamber pots out into the streets at the same time every afternoon."

Paris grimaced at the thought. "I think they might still be doing that here," he said, trying to look any-where but the gutter.

Darrell grinned through her lace handkerchief. "Yeah, I had a few narrow escapes. Talk about being in the wrong place at the wrong time! But don't worry. You'll get used to it."

Though there was no sign of any new greenery on the bare trees, the afternoon sun shone, and there was a hint of warmth in the air. True to his word, between bouts of time sickness, Paris had found a few rough tools in the shed behind the cottage. He had put them to good use and fashioned a walking stick for Darrell out of a fallen branch from a rowan tree.

Darrell threw her cloak back over her shoulders, feeling the warmth of the sun. "Thanks for the cane, Paris," she said gratefully. "It's really helping on these slippery cobbles."

"Sorry I didn't have time to make it look any nicer," he replied.

"It's just fine," she said firmly. "The part where I hold it is so smooth I'm sure I won't get a blister, and the bottom is just rough enough that it keeps me from slipping."

"How is your foot?" asked Paris, curiously. "It looks a lot harder to walk on than that cool machine you wear at home."

Darrell swung the leg forward and put all her weight on it. "Bit creaky, but not bad. You should have seen the peg leg I had to wear in Florence — it looked like someone had sawn it off a piano!"

Paris put a cautious hand on Darrell's arm to stop her, and they watched in wonder as a man, his clothing in shreds, limped down the street in front of them. As he walked, he slapped his own back with a long scourge, and the blood from the wounds trickled down behind him into his footsteps as he staggered away.

"What was that?" Paris's eyes were wide.

Darrell shook her head. "I've only read about it," she whispered. "He must be a flagellant — a person who believes that his own misery can counteract the sins of the world." She wiped her mouth with her handkerchief, still feeling a little faint from the sight.

"A pretty sickening way to get into heaven," said Paris as he steered Darrell back onto the road.

"Not for a true believer, I guess," she replied.

The village high street ended at the gatehouse to the castle, and they stopped there, uncertainly.

It sure looks different than the pictures I've seen, thought Darrell. Windsor Castle, home to the kings and queens of England since the time of William the Conqueror. She quailed a little at the thought of what, or more precisely *who*, they faced inside.

A small soldier, almost a full foot shorter than Paris, stepped out to greet them. His startled look passed from Paris to Darrell, but he addressed his remarks to Paris.

"'Od's blood," he said breathlessly. "Just wait until the commander sees you. Lady Anne tells me you are here to join the castle guard?"

Darrell widened her eyes at Paris and mouthed, "Lady Anne?"

Paris shrugged and turned back to the soldier. "We are here to join the castle staff and help in whatever way we can," he said, glancing at Darrell for her approval. She nodded. "This is — er — my sister, Dara. She is — uh — under my protection."

Darrell glowered down at the small soldier. "I don't need anyone's protection," she hissed belligerently at Paris.

"Yes, miss — I can see that with my own eyes," said the little man. He quickly summoned a pair of small pages. Paris, Delaney trailing at his heel, was sent off to meet the captain of the guard, while Darrell was escorted into the main courtyard for the afternoon petitioners session with the queen.

She stood where the page pointed, near the back of a large room. The walls of the room were hung with heavy tapestries, but the windows were thrown open to catch the spring air.

Several people stood closer to the front of the room, an area dominated by a raised dais. In the centre of a small crowd was a woman with a vast sweep of long hair that, unlike the other women, she kept uncovered.

She was very plump and sat surrounded by her attendants, including Nan, who looked striking in a black
velvet gown and headpiece. Darrell noticed that Nan
wore the same frivolously ruffled gloves that she had
worn the day before. A tiny girl of eight or nine years
sat at the feet of the queen, demurely embroidering a
piece of fabric in a small hoop.

A young man stepped forward from the crowd
before Queen Katherine, twisting his hat nervously in
his hands, and cleared his throat. She nodded her head
at him sagely and he dropped to one knee.

"Beggin' your Majesty's pardon," he said, "but
my wife ailing with the sweats, I felt I had to come
before you and ask that she be spared from her labours
at the castle until she returns to full health, if it be
your pleasure, m'um."

The queen lifted her handkerchief delicately to
her nose.

"That is quite all right, my good man. We have
no wish to have further exposure to that dreadful illness here in the castle. What is your wife's position,
good sir?"

"Why, she works in the kitchen, yer Majesty. She's a
helper to the cooks."

"All the more reason for us to wait cheerily for her
full health to return before she comes back to us." The
queen paused. "And what is your labour, good sir?"

"I works in the smithy, m'um. The smith gave me the time off to come and speak to you today."

"Good man." The queen dropped something into the hand of one of her ladies, who ran forward to hand it to the queen's petitioner. "This is for you and your good lady, young man. And pass a farthing on to your smith, for his kind will in allowing you to appear before me today."

The young man beamed up at the queen. "Lor' bless you mu'm — I — I mean yer Majesty. Thank you most kindly for your charity."

The queen smiled serenely. "The Lord looks fondly upon charitable works, young man. Good day."

Dismissed, he walked backward awkwardly until he reached the rear of the room and then fled, clutching the money given him by the queen like a badge of honour for all to see.

Darrell could see Nan lean forward and whisper in the queen's ear. The queen stiffened but gave a quick nod to Nan.

"Is there a Mistress Dara present?" she called out, her tone more strident than regal.

Darrell swallowed hard and stepped forward.

"Curtsy before her Majesty, the Queen Katherine," hissed the page. Darrell did her best, feeling a bit roughish in the curtsy department.

"Queen — uh — Katherine?" began Darrell.

Beside the queen, Nan Bullen smiled and nodded encouragingly.

Darrell smiled back at Nan. "My brother and I have come from afar, your Majesty, to escape the sickness that swept through our village. When we arrived here we came straight to the castle to offer our humble services."

The monarch nodded gracefully. "Lady Anne has told us your story," she said. "You may know that the dreadful sweating sickness has recently passed through our own court. It is imperative that we replace the courtiers that were taken ill with healthy staff."

Lady Anne? thought Darrell again. *What is Nan up to?*

Queen Katherine raised her hands and two of the ladies who sat by her side immediately leapt up to help their mistress to her feet. She stepped down off the dais and limped heavily over to where Darrell stood. Up close, it was clear she was substantially overweight and appeared to be expecting a baby as well.

Nan stepped down behind the queen. "I think you will find, your Majesty, that the new attendant I have found you is in excellent health."

The queen leaned forward and peered closely into Darrell's face. In addition to her other physical disabilities she was apparently very nearsighted. Darrell's attention was drawn to Nan, still standing behind the queen. She dropped an eyelid and touched her finger to the side of her nose in a cheeky gesture.

"You do appear to be in extremely good health," the queen said, having to look upwards six or eight inches to Darrell's face. "I cannot remember seeing a young lady quite so tall for many years."

"Thank you, your Majesty."

Nan came forward and put a hand on the queen's arm. "This lovely young girl shows no sign of the sweat, dearest lady. And look at her! It's been years since I have seen an attendant in such a bloom of good health. She will be strong as an ox — think what a help she will be!"

Another of the ladies stepped down off the dais. She flared her nostrils at Nan as though a bad smell had swept through the room and walked over to whisper into the ear of the queen. "She appears to be missing a leg, milady. Indeed, as all can witness, it is apparent that she requires a stick in order to walk. 'Od's truth, I believe she walks not upon flesh at all."

The queen peered nearsightedly back at Darrell. "Is this the case, petitioner?"

Darrell lifted her chin and glared at the lady-in-waiting. After a long moment of silence, she spoke. "It is. However," and in two strong strides she crossed the room to stand in front of the whispering lady, "my foot may be of wood, but it serves me well, and I would do the same for this household, m'lady, if you will have me."

The queen tilted her head to one side. "Unlike you, Lady Margaret," and she extended a hand to the whispering lady, "I am inclined to take Lady Anne's word on behalf of this petitioner." She stumbled on the step up to the dais and seated herself with difficulty. "We are inclined to support the cause of this young lady, for she looks to me to be in excellent health and fine spirits. Besides," she turned to Darrell and smiled benignly, "after the recent losses, beggars cannot be choosers. We welcome you!"

"Thank you, your Majesty." Darrell took a deep breath and swept to the ground in a full curtsy that would do any ballerina proud. "Put that in your pipe and smoke it, Lady Margaret," she muttered as she started to walk away.

"Never turn your back on your queen," hissed the page, gesturing wildly.

Darrell spun around quickly, her face flushing at the breach in protocol, but the queen waved her benignly away. "Cannot imagine trying to walk backwards with only one leg," she said jovially to her ladies, who all laughed politely.

Darrell seethed in silence and vowed to master the art of walking backwards with a wooden foot, even if it killed her.

The page ushered Darrell away, and Nan, after whispering a few words and bowing prettily before her queen, hurried after her.

"Queen Katherine has freed me to take you on a tour of the castle," she said, "but you'll see it all soon enough. I have something else to show you. Follow me."

As they walked, Darrell noticed that while many of the men about the castle doffed their hats or even bowed deeply to Nan, the young women were more inclined to turn their backs. "Nan," she said carefully. "I noticed that the queen referred to you as Lady Anne. I am sorry, but I am not aware of your full title …?"

Nan giggled. "I'm afraid I haven't shared that with you, for during the time I spent with Queen Claude in France, I was called Nan, and it is a name I like my true friends to use. But of course in England, everyone knows it is only a nickname for Anne." She dropped into an effortless curtsy, her nose nearly whisking the floor. "I am known as the Lady Anne, daughter of Sir Thomas Boleyn," she said with a dimpled smile.

CHAPTER TEN

"Your brother will be billeted in the stables until room is found for him in the barracks," whispered Anne. "And you shall stay with me. I have a small solar that I share with two others of the queen's ladies, but very soon I will have apartments of my own within the castle."

Darrell nodded, not really listening, and looked around the magnificent chamber in which they sat. St. George's chapel was a stunning room with hugely vaulted ceilings and soaring windows of stained glass. Anne had brought her up to the choir loft for the best view of the beautiful chapel.

"It's only just been finished," said Anne, keeping her voice low. "Henry ordered it to be completed so he and the Knights of the Garter can engage in their ceremonies here." She held Darrell's hand in both of her own. "And it is here that I plan to be married," she whispered.

Darrell smiled politely and tried to think of a way to steer the conversation around to find out more about Friar Priamos. "Will you be married by the friar?" she asked.

Anne arched an eyebrow. "Of course not. He and I only discuss secular matters and changes within the church. No, I will be married by the highest priest in the land, as is befitting a queen!"

Darrell turned her head and pretended to study the detailed architecture. She was running out of energy for Anne's prattling about marriage. She tried a new tactic.

"Perhaps I could meet Friar Priamos," she suggested. "We could talk more of the ideas of Luther."

Anne waved a heavily gloved hand dismissively. "Perhaps." She clutched Darrell's arm. "The king invited me to sit at his court this morning, and he was soon bored of his paperwork." She laughed aloud. "Such a manly man, don't you think?"

Darrell rolled her eyes. "Whatever you say, Lady Anne." This was getting truly boring. Who cared if the king was manly? And why would this young woman care what the king was thinking?

"… a tournament tomorrow! Isn't that wonderful?"

Darrell realized she had missed some of Anne's chatter. "A tournament, did you say?"

"Yes." For the first time, Anne looked a trifle impatient with her new friend. "Aren't you listening? I said that Henry and his courtiers decided to hold a spring tournament." She stood up and dragged Darrell over to a small window that overlooked a huge grass field known as the Lower Ward. The field was a flurry of activity as banners and stands were hastily erected.

Darrell nodded and did her best to appear interested. "It looks like fun," she said with as much enthusiasm as she could muster.

"Oh it will be, indeed. And I have a strong feeling that I shall be asked to sit in the royal box."

Darrell looked closely at Anne. As far as she could remember, the king had no son of marriageable age — no sons at all, as a matter of fact. Darrell knew that the young girl who sat at the feet of the queen must be her daughter, Mary, but try as she might, she couldn't remember who succeeded Henry VIII. Was there a Henry IX, and did Anne have designs on him? "You mentioned a new beau, yesterday, Anne," she asked as they walked back to the kitchens. "Do you plan to marry someone in line for the throne?"

Anne's eyes sparkled, and she gave her most bewitching smile. "I will marry whoever catches my fancy," she said and gave a small pirouette. "For I am known for the magic of my smile."

A great feast was held that evening in preparation for the festivities of the following day, and Darrell quickly learned that an attendant to the queen had many duties to fulfill. Long before the dinner was to begin she was hauled into service in the kitchen and spent what felt like hours setting up the great tables in the dining hall. Anne had sought her out to tell her that since Darrell was now in the direct service of the queen, both she and Paris were invited to dine in the hall with the nobles rather than on leavings in the kitchen with the rest of the servants.

"Now I know how Kate felt when she was stuck in the kitchens in Scotland and Florence," whispered Darrell to Paris. He had spent the afternoon readying the horses for the joust and she had run down to give him the news of the dinner.

"You think that's bad," he said, pushing a stiff brush into Darrell's hand and showing her how to use it. "I've been cleaning out horses' hooves all morning." He rubbed his back ruefully. "You hoist the foot of the horse off the ground and hope that he doesn't lean on you, and then you take this big hook and pick out everything that's caught in his hooves." He wrinkled his nose in disgust. "Ever seen what a horse steps on, Darrell? It isn't pretty."

She grinned at him. "It's good for you, Paris. Anyway, I saw Anne creeping off after bragging to me that she was going to marry big, and I think I know where she went. She is always talking about this friar, but I haven't actually managed to meet him yet." She ran the brush over the smooth, brown coat of the horse. "I really believe he's the key to finding Conrad, Paris. I had hoped that Anne would help, but she's too full of herself and her marriage plans to think about anyone else."

Paris finished brushing the horse's mane and led the beast back into a nearby stall. "Well, let's hope you find Friar Priamos quickly," he said. "I haven't been sick for three hours now, but I'm not sure how much more of this time travel stuff my stomach can take."

"Oh, you must come!"

Anne's eyes shone. She was dressed in an elaborately ruffled gown with gloves reaching up past her elbows. She turned on her heel and, with a rustle of skirts, plunged deep into the cupboard near the scullery door. After a moment there was a muffled shriek of triumph from inside the cupboard. She emerged, brushing a large cobweb from her hair.

"I *knew* I had seen these somewhere!" In one hand she held a slender length of wood, from one end of which dangled a mass of fine cord. In her other hand were a clutch of arrows, none of which looked in terribly good shape to Darrell.

"See? I told you I have tried archery before." Anne was brimming with excitement. She nodded slyly at

Darrell. "You must invite that handsome brother of yours to play rovers. With his height I'm sure he can compete with those who draw the largest of the longbows."

Darrell raised her eyebrows. "I'm not so sure he's feeling up to it. His stomach is still bothering him a little."

Anne fiddled with her gloves at the wrist. "Perhaps I can find a way to help with the problem," she murmured. She thrust the dusty arrows into Darrell's hands and strode over to the window to examine the preparations.

Darrell joined Anne at the window. "Rovers?"

"It is a most wonderful game, with the archers moving from target to target across the field," Anne explained. "Look — there is the first — that large figure painted on the board. The archer closest to the heart of the figure will win that one. And there ..." She gestured farther afield. "See that brightly coloured creature atop the tree? That is the popinjay, and the archer who unseats him from his perch is the winner." They leaned out the window for a moment, watching as the targets were scattered across one section of the large field. "Each target taken means a prize for the winner, and the overall champion might win the king's favour — unless he himself competes, and then the prize might be something else entirely." Anne, catching sight of someone below, blushed slightly and waved her handkerchief.

Darrell looked down to see a tall man striding across the field, bellowing orders. It took her a moment to recognize him, but when she did it was hard to take her eyes off him.

King Henry himself. More than six feet tall in a time when the average male topped out at five foot six, he was an imposing figure. He looked nothing like the pictures Darrell had ever seen of him. He was not overweight so much as he was huge, a giant of a man who had no trouble exerting his own authority. He marched around the field truculently directing the servants as though he were readying for war.

Darrell felt a knot form in her stomach, a mixture of interest and fear, of wonder and loathing as she looked at this man — younger even than her uncle — who wielded so much power in his large fist.

Anne had drawn her fan up over her face and peered over it coquettishly. "I wonder who I should choose for my champion," she mused, her eyes distant and preoccupied. "Perhaps," she glanced at Darrell, "perhaps I shall choose your handsome brother, for surely he will be among the winners."

Darrell, still feeling stunned from her first view of the king, made a remarkable show of feigning indifference. "Suit yourself," she said and turned casually again to look out the window. Banners and flags snapped in a brisk breeze and fine smells floated out the window from the kitchens.

Darrell felt a momentary pang for Paris. When she'd seen him in the stables this morning he had looked pale as paper, and though he said he had not been sick all night, he had not been able to eat anything, either.

"Smells like roast ox," Anne said with a grin. "Henry's favourite."

Darrell thought of Anne's little wave and a slow suspicion began to grow in her mind.

Anne looked at her curiously. "You do not object if I choose your brother for my champion?" she asked.

"Champion? How can Paris be the champion when he has not even participated yet?"

Anne laughed heartily. "You must choose a champion who will take your token," she said. "Bring a silk scarf or a bit of lace handkerchief, and he will tie it to his sleeve and compete in your honour," she explained, as though to a child.

"Perhaps I should be my own champion," said Darrell recklessly. "You have just shown me that you have the arrows. Why can't I compete?"

Anne's jaw dropped and clutched Darrell's arm. "You surely jest."

Darrell laughed and shook her head. "I do not. Where I come from, Lady Anne, I have seen women in circumstances where they would often compete with each other and with men."

Anne picked up the unstrung bow from the table. "But these are just toys, Mistress Dara. Even in games all the equipment used is real."

Darrell tossed her head. "I'm not afraid of playing bows and arrows," she said. "I just need to get myself out of this dress." She plucked impatiently at the laces that threaded down the front of her gown.

Anne looked on for a moment in amazement and then laughed again, loud and long. She turned to Darrell. "Come with me," she demanded, her eyes dancing with mischief. "I believe this day will bring a new sort of champion to Henry's court."

CHAPTER ELEVEN

The tournament began with a near royal tragedy. The first event of the day was the joust, and the competition was well underway. The king competed enthusiastically in a new suit of armour of his own design. Darrell, now dressed in castle livery with her hair tucked into a cap, stood nervously with Paris on the sidelines of the jousting lists. People from all around the town of Windsor and the neighbouring villages crowded into the lower ward to watch the contests.

Paris was also dressed in the castle livery and held an unstrung bow of some six feet in length.

"I haven't eaten anything in days," he said weakly. "There is no way I'm going to be able to shoot this thing."

"Something tells me you are going to have another role to play today if Anne has anything to do with it," hissed Darrell. "Besides, I plan to make short work of the competition with my fancy archery skills."

"That calls for a drink," said Paris, "since you've probably never drawn a bow in your life." He pulled out a small flask and took a tentative sip.

"What on earth is that?" asked Darrell, alarmed. Behind her, the horse thundered by and with a deafening crash one of the jousters was unseated. A roar went up from the crowd.

"Lady Anne gave it to me," he said. "I don't know what's in it, and it tastes just horrible, but I haven't been sick all afternoon."

Darrell nodded sympathetically. She looked up to the stands where the nobility sat in a tapestry-draped section. Anne was deep in conversation with a hooded figure in a scarlet cloak.

Darrell nudged Paris. "Look! Can you make out who Anne is talking to?"

Paris shrugged. "No. Too far away."

Darrell craned her neck. "It must be Friar Priamos. Anne is up to something. I need to talk with that man before she gets him caught up in some kind of scheme."

She hurried over towards the stands just as the final joust began. The horses thundered toward each other, and a gasp went up from the crowd. Darrell, who had decided right away that she was not at all fond of jousting, looked up instinctively. She was just in time to see the lance of one horseman smash into the open visor of the other.

Shouts of "The king is down" resounded across the field, and the entire crowd fell silent. Darrell hopped up on a fencepost to crane over the sea of heads.

A single cry rang out. "He stands!"

The crowd roared their approval. Darrell hopped off the fence and hurried over to the royal box. Anne, her face troubled, leaned over the edge of the box, gesturing toward the newly re-horsed competitors.

Darrell noticed that the queen was not anywhere to be seen in the royal stands.

"Just a scratch, worry not," called the king to the nobles in the stands. He waved to the crowd, who once again cheered resoundingly. Darrell could hear the other knight babbling. "A thousand apologies, your highness, I did not see your visor was not firmly in place."

The king turned his head, and Darrell could see where the point of the lance had opened up a small wound beside his eye. "A scratch only, my dear Suffolk. Think nothing of it. I am well and ready to joust again."

While the courtiers tried to talk Henry out of his armour, Darrell sidled up through the stands to Anne. The cloaked figure was nowhere to be seen.

Anne smiled with relief when she spied Darrell. "He is well, with little damage done," she reported. "And your livery suits you, young sir," she whispered with a grin.

"I was wondering ..." began Darrell.

"Milady, a token, perhaps?" Darrell spun around to find herself face to face with King Henry, who had ridden to the royal box and leaned inside, still mounted. The saliva in her mouth suddenly dried up.

Anne rewarded the king with one of her dazzling smiles. "I had been about to give my token to this archer," she said coquettishly.

Darrell raised her eyebrows in alarm.

The king snorted. "You would choose a common archer over your liege and ruler of all the land?" he asked, carefully turning his face so as best to expose the wound.

"Never, my lord!" declared Anne, and she made a show of pulling a lace handkerchief from her dress and tying it around the king's arm. The soft cloth slid down to his wrist, and with a final grin to Anne he galloped back to the middle of the field waving her token at the still-cheering crowd.

Meanwhile, the courtiers had begun to dismantle the jousting lists to make way for the archery competition, so the disappointed king finally dismounted. His voice could be heard over the crowd insisting that he could compete again and would, in fact, challenge any man present to prove himself. To Darrell's relief, everyone had the sense to keep quiet, and the call for the archery competition soon rang out.

Anne pushed through the crowd to stand between Paris and Darrell as the crier bellowed the order of the targets for the competition.

"Wasn't that exciting?" she said quietly. "And did you see how the king took my favour — mine?"

It was just at that moment that something clicked into place in Darrell's memory. "Anne Boleyn," she said aloud without thinking. "I remember now — you are to marry the king!"

Anne beamed at her. "It is my fondest hope," she whispered. "And I hope to convince Friar Priamos to work with those that have the ear of the pope. Henry plans to have his marriage to Katherine annulled and to marry me in her stead."

Darrell shook her head. "Isn't the queen going to have another baby soon? What if she has a boy?"

Anne shrugged. "The queen was delivered of a still-born child yesterday," she said with a coldness that shocked Darrell. "It was that event that has brought Henry to make up his mind at last. It is his fondest desire to annul the marriage to Katherine. She is barren, and I am to be queen!"

Darrell sighed inwardly. If Anne was to be married, she would never have time to help find Conrad. She clutched Anne's arm. "I must speak with the friar," she pleaded. "I believe he can tell me of the person I seek — someone who once assisted Brother Socorro."

Anne sniffed. "I thought you were interested in the teachings of Luther," she said curtly. "I thought you cared about the changes that are taking place in the church, changes that may well open the way for me to be queen." She turned her back, glancing just once over her shoulder. "Friar Priamos is too busy to see you," she said. "And you have a contest to enter."

Just then a voice called out from the crowd. "The horses! A group of lads are stealing the horses!" Suddenly all was chaos. Anne melted away into the crowd, and Darrell and Paris found themselves being hustled across the field along with the other footmen in pursuit of the horse thieves.

Darrell clung to Paris's arm. "I can't chase down horse thieves," she gasped. "I can hardly walk without my stick."

"You there — come with me." Darrell watched as Paris, with a last helpless glance in her direction, was yanked away into a group of men who charged out of the castle gates and down into the surrounding forest.

Darrell felt frantic. None of this was going as planned. Paris was weak from having not eaten for days and had been suddenly sent off with a group of young men, rabid for the blood of horse thieves. Anne was preoccupied with winning the heart of a married king, and Darrell was no closer to finding Conrad after two full days than she had been when they arrived.

She limped back into the castle and found her walking stick tucked in a corner of one of the kitchens. Around her, preparations for the post-tournament feast were well underway. Darrell walked though the dining hall in the round tower and glanced up to see Anne walking with a figure, this time in a blue cloak.

Darrell dashed to the stairs, but was thwarted by guards. "Above stairs is closed, young sir," said the guard, and Darrell realized she was still wearing the castle livery. "The queen is ill and will abide no interference at this time," the guard added.

Darrell nodded and turned on her heel. Perhaps it was better to let Anne cool down a little, anyway. And right now, she needed to make sure Paris hadn't been pulled into more trouble than he could handle.

Paris lifted his head groggily and tried to get his bearings. The air was smoke-filled and still, with any sounds of turmoil fading far into the distance. He felt nauseated and hollow. He tried to roll over and sit up, but found his legs were pinned tightly to the ground. It took him a moment to realize that there was a person lying on his legs — or what used to be a person.

The sight of the dead body draped across him brought nausea rolling through his gut again. Panicked that he couldn't get free, he tried to kick his legs, to no avail. In the end, he pulled himself away by wedging a sword he yanked out of the dead man's hands against his weight.

As the blood rushed back into his legs, Paris felt as though insects were crawling under his torn woollen trousers. Still panicky, he scrabbled sideways, crab-like, the mud squelching up between his fingers in a thick paste. He stopped only when his shoulder made painful contact with the ragged stump of a tree. Wiping his hands as best he could, Paris closed his eyes and leaned his head back against the stump.

He remembered running with the group of foot soldiers and then being tackled from behind. After that, things seemed fuzzier.

Aside from the dead man a few feet away, the main problem seemed to be the smell. The wide variety of strong odours hadn't helped his nausea throughout the journey, but right now there was no escaping the sick-sweet stench. He felt like it had been in the air for days, but at a distance, somehow, like something rotten in the next yard. But the sudden turn of events had brought the reek of death into pinpoint clarity, and once again panic rose in his throat.

It was time to find Darrell and get back to Eagle Glen. He'd been sick for days and willing to put up with it, but now this had happened. Suddenly the journey no longer seemed such an adventure.

From the deepening chill, Paris could tell night wasn't far away. He needed to find his way back to the castle before darkness set in.

He glanced back at the man he had been trapped beneath, the body stiffening in the grotesque rictus of death. Paris stared at the corpse, his eyes glazed and tired, trying to fathom why this body that minutes or hours before had been a living, breathing creature — why had this man seen fit to try to kill him? The man was dressed in simple peasant's garb, and the sword that he had carried lay unbroken beside him in the mud.

Paris stood up at last and walked back to the body. A broken dagger Paris had not noticed before lay next to the man's hand. The horse thief lay face down in the mud, the back of his russet jacket now black with the blood that had muddied the ground where he lay.

Paris was filled with a sudden anger against this stranger who had tried to take his life. He felt an overwhelming desire to kick the body that lay prone in the mud, but instead dropped to his knees and grabbed the man by the shoulders, intent on turning the body over.

Already starting to stiffen and weighed down with a thick leather vest, the body was heavier than Paris had expected. It took several seconds to wrest the man onto his back.

Paris's hands felt glued to the thief's shoulders as he stared blankly into the dead face. There was no mark to be seen there, no scratch or scrape or bruise. Just a smudge of mud on the cheek. In shock, Paris, his anger drained, pulled his hands away. Milky eyes were open and seemed to be staring at him from a face that belonged to a boy of fourteen or perhaps fifteen years. A boy Paris's own age, now dead after trying to steal a horse.

Suddenly, Paris thought of his own mother, and how she would feel if someone had to tell her of his own death. A pain as sharp as the dagger below him coursed through his heart.

He bent over and gently closed the eyes of the dead boy. He looked around for something with which to cover him and found nothing. Instead, he took the broken dagger and placed it in the boy's hands on his chest. He closed his eyes briefly and wished himself to be anywhere but in these woods, so far from his own home. He stepped, swaying, to his feet and heard a shout.

"All right, mate?"

He spun around to look behind and saw one of the castle's foot soldiers approaching. "I'm fine," he said, with a sudden surge of relief that this was indeed the truth.

"Yer name is Paris, innit?" The foot soldier looked down and spat on the body. "Filthy thief, trying to steal the king's good horseflesh," he muttered. "Got what he deserved, he did." He looked up at Paris. "Yer sister's looking for ya. She'll be up at the castle, worryin' over ya. You head back to see her — I'll deal with this thing."

Paris nodded, too exhausted to protest. The foot soldier flipped the body of the dead boy over his shoulder with a grunt and led Paris back through the Windsor woods.

Darrell had searched frantically for most of the evening and finally spotted Paris following a foot soldier through the edge of the forest. She was horrified by his story.

"Looks like we were both spending time contemplating your death," she said, as they wandered back to the castle.

"Yeah. It was a little too close for comfort," said Paris. "I keep thinking about that kid. He looked like he was my age."

Darrell paused with her hand on the outer wall of the Salisbury Tower. "People live very short, hard lives here," she said, quietly. "Did you know that the queen lost a baby this week?"

Paris shook his head. "No — that's awful. When I was out in the woods, I kept thinking of how my mother would feel if someone had to tell her I'd died today. It makes me sick to think of it."

"I guess these days it's more common for women to lose their babies," said Darrell. "Even the children of kings and queens are not really safe. And way more mothers die when they give birth, too."

"I think we don't really understand how good our lives really are compared to everything these people lived through," said Paris quietly. "I sure didn't get it before I saw all this."

Darrell clutched Paris by the arm. "I hate to admit it," she said with a sigh, "but I am beginning to realize that Brodie and Kate were right. I need to know more about this time before I can figure out where to look for Conrad. I feel like he is just within reach, but I can't put my finger on just where to look. Anne is too wrapped up in capturing the fancy of the king, and I can't stop worrying about you. Maybe it's a lost cause after all."

"Well, quit worrying about me," said Paris. "I won't get involved in anything risky like that again. And I haven't been sick all day, thanks to Anne's magic potion, so I'm going to try to eat a little something tonight, okay?"

"Okay." Darrell smiled and they walked in through the newest castle gate, named for King Henry himself. "But after dinner tonight, I'm going to ask Anne for directions back to the cottage in the woods."

CHAPTER TWELVE

Darrell sat bolt upright in the darkness, adrenaline coursing through her. "Who's there?"

"It is only me, Nan," came the whispered reply.

Darrell felt a moment of surprise. Nan — not Anne?

"I'm here to take you back to the cottage," whispered Anne. "I've decided to go with you. I need to go there to clear away some things for Friar Priamos, and I do not want to be seen, so we will have an adventure in the dark together."

Darrell rubbed her eyes and tried to think but her brain refused to come up with any good way to keep Anne at the castle.

"I know you planned to go on the morrow, but I begin to fear those in league with Katherine. Her ladies plot against me and against their king. I realize now that I must remove any items that might link me to Brother Socorro, so they cannot discredit my good name."

Darrell still felt muddle-headed. "But what can they use against you?"

"There are certain items stored at the cottage. I will feel safer when they are in the hands of Friar Priamos, if he will have them."

Darrell quickly realized that Anne was not to be dissuaded from her goal, so she donned her wooden foot and followed Anne out the door.

"I apologize for not treating your concerns seriously," said Anne, in a formal tone. "Friar Priamos has decided he cannot help me in my quest to become queen. He is leaving Henry's court to pursue his calling with the less fortunate." She shook her head in disbelief.

"Might I not speak with the friar himself?" asked Darrell desperately.

"Friar Priamos chooses those with whom he will speak," said Anne, sounding defeated. "I had hoped he would intercede with those who have influence on the pope on my behalf, but that hope has faded."

They made their way carefully down the back stairs and into the servants' quarters. Darrell looked around the dim corridors curiously. None of the opulence of the open areas was in evidence here, with simple plaster walls and plain stone floors instead of the heavy gilt and tapestry to be found upstairs.

They walked quietly through to the stables, and Anne shook one of the small grooms awake to help her saddle a horse. "Go get your brother," she said curtly. "For this will be my final trip to the cottage, and if you would have me as a guide this will be your only chance."

Darrell found Paris asleep curled around Delaney in a pile of straw next to the horse he had been grooming earlier. Delaney stretched and yawned pinkly at Darrell in the light of the small oil lamp. She bent down to pat him.

"I've hardly seen you these last few days, boy," she whispered.

"Oh, he's been having a good time all right," said Paris with a tired smile. "Just today I saw him trailing behind that priest who wears the scarlet robe. They looked like they were getting on like best friends."

Darrell grabbed Paris by the shoulders and gave him a shake. "That's the priest I have been trying to talk to," she said with exasperation. "I can't believe the dog has access to Friar Priamos and I don't."

Anne slipped up behind them. "Friar Priamos never wears a scarlet robe," she said quietly. "It must have been the *Monsignore* you saw. The friar always dresses in grey — he is a Franciscan — a Grey Friar." She reached down to pat the dog, and for the first time, Darrell noticed that she wasn't wearing gloves. The gleam of a second nail on the smallest finger of her right hand was evident in the light.

Anne caught her glance and tucked her hand farther into her sleeve. "So now you share my secret," she said, her voice low. "When I first saw your injured leg, it drew me to you. I find I prefer people and things that do not smack of perfection."

Darrell laughed quietly. "You are right to appreciate me, then," she said. "Because I'm full of flaws. One of the worst is persistence, and that's why I've been bothering you so much about Friar Priamos."

Anne and the sleepy groom led the horses out into the yard. "We are much alike, Dara," she said. "You must ride behind me for our nighttime adventure."

Darrell swallowed and tried to forget her limited horseback riding experience.

"Hello my beauty," Anne crooned, stroking her horse. "Can you mount?" she asked, turning back to Darrell.

"I think so." Darrell reached for the horn of the saddle but, to her dismay, found none.

"Just take hold of the mane," whispered Anne. "The groom and I will do the rest."

She was a pretty mare, completely black with a single white crest at her brow, the better to blend perfectly into the darkness. Darrell put her foot on the groom's bended knee, and Anne flung her bodily over the back of the horse before hopping nimbly up in front of her passenger. The groom helped Anne adjust herself into the sidesaddle, and Darrell clung on behind.

Paris climbed onto his horse with difficulty. "Are you sure about this?" he said as the horses plodded out of the yard and down the hill toward the forest.

Anne nodded. "We can get there in no time with the horses, the better to avoid long noses and prying eyes," she said, and her white teeth gleamed in the dark. "You are far too old to have so much worry over the control of a horse." Leaning over, she gave Paris's mount a resounding slap. The horse rose slightly onto its hind legs, and Darrell had a quick glimpse of Paris's horror-stricken face as his mount galloped down the hill.

The pretty black mare soon caught up, and they continued at a slower pace, much to Darrell's relief. The path through the woods wound tightly around a few sharp curves and then thrust like a tongue straight through the trees. Night still wrapped her velvet cloak around them, but Darrell could see the outline of trees overhead. Morning was not long off.

Anne led the beast through the trees at a brisk walk while Darrell clung to Anne with her arms and the horse with her legs. Paris, barely recovered from his gallop, rode behind them holding on for dear life.

After fifteen minutes or so of riding, Darrell began to get a bit of a feel for the horse underneath her and risked breaking her concentration to ask a question. "Why are there no bushes or low undergrowth beneath these trees?"

"This land is all the property of King Henry," Anne replied proudly. "The lands are kept clear so that the king and his nobles may hunt more easily. 'Tis unfortunate that the way is also made clearer for those who would hunt us."

"But why are we of interest to anyone?"

"The hold of the church is very strong, especially in these smaller villages. Anyone offering aid to those of other beliefs is severely dealt with. I even worry that members of my family are not to be trusted. My uncle, the Duke of Norfolk, would do much for power. He introduced me to Henry, but I still fear the look in his eye." Clutching the reins with one hand, Anne crossed herself.

"Could Friar Priamos be in danger?" said Darrell.

Anne nodded, and her eyes glinted in the dark. "If these items that I have hidden are connected with his name. There are those in court who would celebrate my downfall. Remember Brother Socorro lost his life for defying the Catholic Church. I am not sure if the reforms which Luther calls for will ever be seen in my lifetime, and I realize now that Henry must work within the constraints of the church to gain his freedom from Katherine."

Moments later the horse trotted into the muddy yard in front of the familiar cottage. Anne swung down from the horse and, surprisingly, turned to help Darrell down as well.

Paris slid off his own mount with an expression of immense relief. Delaney capered around his heels, exhilarated by the nighttime run.

They walked inside and waited until Anne lit a small oil lamp. She held up the light to illuminate the contents of the small corner closet, and Darrell noticed the faintest red outline of the charred falcon symbol on the wooden doorframe. She shot a nervous glance at Paris.

"Here are the ledgers," said Anne. "Socorro asked me to pass them on to Friar Priamos, but as he has decided not to help me now, I wonder if you would have them."

She placed three leather volumes into Darrell's hands. Darrell opened the back cover of the largest and saw where a page had been torn out. "Two of these belonged to Brother Socorro," she said. "I have seen them before."

Anne held up the small menorah that Darrell had last seen in the hands of Brother Socorro as he was taken away by soldiers in Portugal. "I don't know why he wants to keep this silly thing — I'm not even sure it is made of real gold," she muttered.

Darrell examined the ledgers in her hands. Three — why three?

"Do you want to keep them?" demanded Anne. "Otherwise I must turn them over to the friar. It was Socorro's wish that they be kept safe, and now with those loyal to Katherine stirring against me, it is better if I rid myself of the burden."

"But what about Friar Priamos?" asked Paris.

Anne gave an unladylike snort. "He tells me that his life is now to be devoted to helping those in need. But what about me? I am in need, as is his king — in need of help from the pope. The friar seems to think that he can have no influence in this situation, and he has washed his hands of us. Socorro would never have done this to me. The books are yours if you want them, as a memory of him."

A horse whinnied outside the cottage, and Delaney growled low in his throat. "I have never seen this volume before," said Darrell slowly. She slipped open the cover and scanned the first page, then looked over at Paris, her eyes wide. He was examining the notebook with the russet cover.

"Lady Anne. Perhaps you would care to explain why you find yourself here in this nasty little hovel with such unsavoury company?"

Darrell looked up through the doorway to see a woman she remembered as one of Katherine's ladies. Lady Margaret was being lifted lightly off her horse by the captain of the guard. Darrell quickly slid the smallest book into one of the pockets of her skirt.

As Anne turned to the door, she slipped the menorah into a pocket of her own. "I have come to bid farewell to these travellers," she said smoothly. "They have received word from their family that all is once again well in their small village. The sweating sickness has passed and they are returning home. They are merely gathering the last of their possessions before departure."

Lady Margaret shook her head disbelievingly. "Do you take me for a fool, Anne? I have watched for months as that filthy friar has been spiriting people in and out of this cottage in the dark of night. I knew in my heart you must be involved in some manner."

She strolled over to Paris and plucked a volume from his hand. "I believe I'll just take this ledger," she said sharply. "For if it is evidence of any sort of treasonous behaviour on your part, Anne, your hopes for stealing the king from Queen Katherine will be soon dashed."

Anne shot a warning glance over her shoulder at Darrell. "You are far too fond of Katherine, Margaret. The king is poised to cast her aside when the annulment comes through from Rome. She is barren, unable to mother a male heir to the throne. One day it will be my chance to do just that."

"That chance will not come if you are shown to be supporting heretics over the Church," spat Lady Margaret. "Perhaps these ledgers will be your undoing."

She whirled to face the door. "Guard! Arrest these two strangers at once." She looked up into Darrell's startled face. "I knew you were up to mischief from the moment I saw you," she said in a low voice. "Your deformity is a mark of the devil, as is the one carried by that witch. I will live to see you rot in the Tower as a heretic before God."

Darrell locked her gaze on Paris, and he swallowed audibly. "Just let us say goodbye to our dog," he said. "Here, boy!"

And before the startled eyes of Anne, Margaret, and the captain of the castle guard, Paris clasped Darrell's hand tightly. The two travellers and their dog stepped through the low closet doorway and into the thundering winds of time.

CHAPTER THIRTEEN

Darrell sat on her bed at school, staring out the great curved window as the rain coursed down the glass in torrents. She held a small and very old book between her knees.

"The chief disadvantage to living in a temperate rainforest is that it frequently seems to be raining," Kate muttered as she climbed out from under her covers for her blurry first look at the day. "I thought you were spending the whole weekend with your uncle," she said. "Did you shop the entire city out and have to come back early?"

The joke died on her lips when she looked over at Darrell's grief-stricken face.

"I didn't kill him," she whispered quietly. "I just sent him to hell."

Kate rubbed her eyes and looked at Darrell again.

"You went back?" she asked, pulling one of her blankets up around her shoulders.

Darrell nodded. "Took Paris with me, by mistake."

"What? You took Paris? How did that happen?"

"He knew something was up after we disappeared down in the tunnels under the school that time. I never realized how much he missed Conrad — and I guess Paris listened in on enough conversations to know that I knew something about Conrad's whereabouts. So he waited in the library every night for about a week knowing I might try to sneak away. When he tackled me through the doorway, we ended up there together." She smiled a little. "I was going a little farther away than he'd realized, I guess. He spent the whole time barfing, though, so I don't think he'll be doing any time travel again in the near future."

Kate took one look at the dark circles beneath her friend's eyes and climbed out of bed. She pulled a sweatshirt on over her PJs. "You'd better come with me," she said, stuffing her feet into runners. "We'll go find Brodie and Paris and maybe a latte and you can tell us all about it." She threw a hoodie on over the eclectic outfit and pulled Darrell up off the bed.

"So how did you send Paris to hell?" Kate asked as they settled into chairs in a quiet corner of the dining hall.

She had her hands wrapped around a big cup of caffeine and had added a pair of sweatpants before going to wake Brodie and a very groggy Paris. The dining hall was almost deserted, with most students choosing to sleep in on a Saturday morning.

"I didn't go to hell," said Paris smugly. He was sitting with the remains of an enormous breakfast on the tray in front of him, and Darrell was pleased to see a little colour in his face. He bent over and whispered, "I went to England. And not only that, I'm planning to go again."

"Maybe your next visit should be by airplane," said Darrell dryly.

"Listen, you guys. No matter what Darrell says, that was the most amazing experience of my life. I can't believe that you've all been doing this for so long and I knew nothing about it."

Kate glared at Paris. "Can you keep it down? The reason we've been able to do this is that we *know how to keep our mouths shut*," she hissed.

Paris grinned, unperturbed, and lowered his voice. "So — you wanna hear who we met? Henry the Big-Wig Eighth, that's who!" He looked around the table triumphantly.

Kate cast a wary glance at Darrell. "Something tells me this is not all fun and games," she said in a low voice. "Who did you send to hell, Darrell?"

"Conrad," she said simply and pushed the diary across the table to Kate.

October 12, 1519

This is a hard day. It always is, and has, I must admit, grown a bit easier over the years, but it still wearies. So, with no fear that anyone will ever be able to decipher it, I'm going to do what my patron has suggested so often in the time we have spent together and write some of it down. I have written nothing more than my name for sixteen years, and already my hand aches from the unfamiliar feel of the pen. But as there is no one alive who will ever be able to understand more than a few of the words I write and certainly no one to criticize my spelling or syntax, I will do as Brother Socorro suggests. I doubt it will bring me peace — but perhaps less pain, and that is something.

Even with this simple start my hand aches. For today, that will have to be enough. I have many other duties to attend to. No one in the monastery knows or could possibly care that, not accounting for a minor five-hundred-year glitch in the middle, it is my thirty-second birthday today. An anniversary of sorts. I have lived as long in this century as in the one into which I was born.

"Conrad was thirty-two when he wrote that?" Brodie shook his head. "It's hard to even think it could be true. And I'm sorry, but those words don't sound like him at all."

Darrell shrugged. "I know, the language sounds pretty formal, but you have to remember that he was writing this after learning to speak a form of the language he didn't know before, *and* he'd been speaking that way for sixteen years. Besides, people change. When you have a chance to read more of this, you'll see what he has been through."

"How did you get this thing?" said Brodie, gesturing at the worn and ancient notebook.

"Anne Boleyn had it — she got it from Brother Socorro." Darrell turned to Paris. "I was right, you know. When you read the diary, you'll see. It was Socorro who found Conrad and pulled him out of a madhouse."

She dropped her head into her hands. "I sent him to a madhouse," she said, her voice muffled. "I sent him into hell."

Kate patted Darrell on the shoulder. "Okay, enough of the dramatics, as my mother would say. I really want to hear what happened. Now Paris tackled you through the doorway — then what?"

"It was more of a push with a twist," Paris interjected modestly.

Kate glared at him. "I want to hear this from Darrell," she said sternly. "You'll have time to explain yourself later."

Paris shrank back in his seat, chastened.

Darrell leaned forward. "Well, the portal brought us through to Windsor Castle in England during the early sixteenth century. The biggest problem was that the longer I was there, the more I realized you and Brodie were right. I just didn't have enough information about the time period." she shook her head. "I even forgot who Anne Boleyn was."

"It didn't help that we were introduced to her as Nan Bullen," said Paris practically. "I haven't taken any history at all except for what Gramps has taught us this year, so I didn't know any of this stuff."

"Everyone knows that Henry the Eighth had six wives," said Darrell scathingly. "I can't believe I didn't put it all together until I saw the king himself."

Brodie gave a low whistle. "Now there's a man I would've liked to meet," he said. "One of the most powerful men in the history of the world. Changed the face of religion and politics forever.

"Was he fat?" asked Kate. "He's always fat in the pictures I've seen."

Darrell shook her head. "No, but he wasn't that old yet. I think he was just in his late thirties when we saw him. He was really big though — remember how small the people were as a rule?"

Kate nodded. "I wonder if it's just a myth that he was so big and fat."

"I don't think so," said Darrell. "The man sure loved to eat. We were there for two feasts and the food was amazing."

"Uh — I didn't really enjoy that part," admitted Paris.

Brodie looked at him with interest. "So you were sick for the entire trip? Must be some kind of time sickness, maybe like motion sickness in a car or a boat. How long were you there?"

"Three or four days," said Paris. "Cool how we were only gone for a few hours from here, though."

Brodie nodded. "That's how it usually seems to work. Time compresses as it passes somehow, so when you travel, the proportion goes off. You can seem to be there for a long time and only a few minutes or hours pass here."

"Okay, we know all that," said Kate, impatiently. She clutched Darrell's sleeve. "What do you know now that you didn't before?"

Darrell paused to think for a moment. "I guess I know that I have to read more of this book to find out what happened to Conrad," she said. "The next time I go back, I don't want to make so many stupid mistakes. If I'd known Nan was Anne Boleyn and remembered who she was going to marry, I might have at least figured out where we were a little sooner."

"So — do you think she was a witch?" asked Kate, with a glance over her shoulder.

Darrell shook her head.

"She made a mean time sickness potion for me," said Paris. "It was the only thing that kept my stomach steady the whole time I was there."

Darrell shrugged. "That just means she could have had a simple knowledge of natural medicine. We've had plenty of experience showing how women who had basic medical knowledge were often treated as witches."

"But I read she had six fingers and a giant mole on her neck," said Kate. "More exaggeration?"

Darrell nodded. "She wasn't really a great beauty, but she wasn't a monster, either."

"She sure had a way of looking at you that made you feel she was beautiful," said Paris.

Brodie grinned at him. "Caught your eye, did she?"

"Speaking of eyes — hers were almost pure black," said Paris. "And they kind of sparkled when she laughed and her teeth were really good — whiter than most, I'd say." He wrinkled his nose at Darrell. "I think that's one thing I'll never take for granted again," he added. "Good dental care is worth it. I don't think I've ever seen so many missing and black teeth in my life. And the breath of some of those people!"

"Made all those years in braces worth it, eh, Paris?"

He shrugged. "I only wore braces for two years," he admitted, "but I'll think more kindly of dentists from now on!"

"Listen you guys, I'm really tired," said Darrell, standing up. "I'm going to go have a bit of a nap. We can talk about this more later, okay?" She picked up the book and trudged out of the room.

"She looks really beaten up," said Brodie quietly.

Kate nodded. "I hate to see her this depressed. I think we need to keep a close eye on her for a while."

"Anybody want to hear my English accent?" asked Paris, grinning around the table.

> October 25, 1519
> It's been hard for me to pick up my pen to write as my days are so full. No, that is a lie. I really just don't want to remember, and on top of that I don't want to go to the trouble associated with remembering to write in a language I haven't spoken for so many

years. It was always hard for me to write. I hated school. Always in the lowest class, with the other kids who hated school, too.

One school was different, and I was only there long enough to mess things up.

November 16, 1519

This is worse than I ever thought it would be. Part of me does not want to remember. There's nothing I can do about it, anyway. And what is there to go back to, even if I could? Brother Socorro says that I should write about my present if my past is so painful. My sadness will stay inside if I keep it there.

Here is something I remember that doesn't hurt.

> How to Make Chocolate Chip Cookies
>
> Mix a cup of butter with 2 eggs and 2 cups of sugar. Add vanilla and then mix into a bowl with 2 cups of flour, a teaspoon of baking soda. and a large pinch of salt. Add a

whole pack of chocolate chips
and bake ten minutes in a 350
degree oven.
Hmm. That did hurt after all.
I guess because even though there
are ovens here, and even occasional
sweets, chocolate chips are not going to
exist for at least four hundred years.

For the first time since picking up the old notebook, Darrell laughed a little. *At least he was able to
make a joke now and then*, she thought. Leaning down
beside the bed, she gave Delaney a little pat and then
returned to her reading. She had never in her life so
desperately wanted to know how a story ended.

December 1, 1519
Brother Socorro. Though I know his
face much better than I do my own, it is
still strange to look into his eyes. The
good brother tries to teach me to trust
and one day I may do so without pain. I
can only hope.
So, I will take his advice and write of
my life right now. I spend my days labour-
ing in a monastery. It is an old stone
Abbey, near Blois, in France. The broth-

ers who make their home here have accepted me, mostly because of Brother Socorro. In the winters I work on the river, collecting fish for the brethren. In summer, my job is harvesting not the waters but the gardens, where I labour under the steely eye of Pere Hortus from prime until vespers.

And speaking of such — the bell tolls for Compline and after that, to bed.

December 3, 1519
Only two days have passed and I am drawn once again to this journal. It does bring a strange sort of peace, but perhaps only as a rest from the labours of gutting fish. My knife is sharp and the job is swift, but I tire of cutting heads, slicing bellies, and pulling guts. I hated to write a word at school, since I did so poorly, but now it begins to offer a weird relief for me, and allows me to think of my past, so far in the future.

I've decided to write today of the bells, since the ringing drew me away before. The bells call the brethren to prayer eight times each day starting with

Matins at midnight. Lauds follows at 3:00 a.m., Prime at 6:00 a.m., and Terce at 9:00 a.m. At noon there are the bells for Sext, None is at 3:00 p.m., Vespers at 6:00 p.m., and Compline marks bedtime at 9:00 p.m. The names are drawn from the canonical hours and are named for the prayers that are said at each time of the day. These are a devout people, though it is usually only the friars who fall to their knees so often in the day. Regular folk, even within the sound of the bells, usually pray a mere four or five times daily.

The passage of time holds much fascination for me now, naturally. I will never know how it was that I passed through the wall of time. I know it was a mistake. And I know that in the style I had learned so well from my father, I made things worse. But was I meant to be here in this time?

The bell rings again. Matins. And of course here in the monastery, practicality rules all. Here's something I remember from the past: Time flies when you're having fun.

Christmas, 1519

The day is so different and yet so much the same as the one I knew as a child. Was I ever a child? For a short while, perhaps, before my father had good use to put me to. Through the passage of years I now know he was a hard man. Not a just man. And perhaps not as hard as some.

Christmas here is little different than a regular day. Much praying and for some, a fast. No feasting to be had — that is saved for the feast of St. Stephen, which falls on the following day, December 26. A shade different than the commercial twenty-first-century holiday that I remember. Not that I ever had a lot of toys or candy. I do remember a Tonka truck my mother gave me one Christmas. There was, of course, no Santa Claus in our apartment. No chimney, I always thought, but now I realize there was no magic. No acknowledgement that things could ever be not as they appeared. The Tonka was a yellow dump truck. I kept it for years. I can't seem to remember anything else that was all mine.

Until the dog.

January 4, 1520

Another year. I've put off writing because, as it turns out, I don't really want to remember the dog. He was mine for a few days when he was a puppy. I didn't see him again for three or four years, and by then he was hers. He knew me, but I pretended I didn't know him. I hated everything then. Everything except my dad. I did all I could to get my dad to care about me. Even gave up the puppy. It still didn't work.

Again, this is making things worse, so back to the present.

Today I walked through the village down to the fishing boat. Most of the folk here either make their living on the land or the river. A kind farmer offered me a ride on his cart and I travelled to the market in style, among the wooden crates of chickens.

There is much kindness here, though I did not see it for many years after my abrupt arrival. In my fear after the fire I saw only madness and war and death. And that, I'm happy to say, is for another day.

Darrell slid off the bed and put her arms around Delaney's neck. "I never knew," she whispered. "I never knew you belonged to Conrad, boy. All the time, to think he wanted you so much — he just wanted his dad to love him even more."

> February 17, 1520
> These bleak, dark winter days are filled with work and sleep and little else. The truth is, I have put off writing about my arrival here to push away the sickening memories, but they haunt my dreams still. Brother Socorro suggests I write them and lock them in these pages so as to clear my sleep, and I hope he is right. My childhood was harsh but it prepared me well for what I should find when hauled back through time and so — perhaps — I survived because of hard lessons learned under the hand of my father.

Darrell read on, as Conrad wrote of escaping the fire in the stable only to be dragged away and sold into servitude as a soldier in the Franco-Italian wars. She read as he talked of trying to convince someone — anyone — that he was from another place and another

time. And finally, of his sentence in the worst hell of all
— a medieval madhouse.

The book finished in the middle of a page dated
1523 — a few months before Darrell and Paris arrived
on their short trip through time. Her face wet with
tears, she closed the book carefully. "Your story is not
over yet, Conrad," she whispered. "I promise you'll
have another chance."

CHAPTER FOURTEEN

Spring arrived, and with it came the obligatory break from school. Before leaving for Kate's house, Darrell received a brief call from the Middle East.

"This is such an incredible part of the world, Darrell. This tiny country is where Africa, Asia, and Europe all meet, in a way."

"But what about the war, Mom? Are you in danger?"

Janice Connor's voice buzzed through the phone. "I won't pretend this is always a safe place, Darrell. But I promise you that David and I are doing our best to keep each other out of trouble."

David and I. Darrell sighed and decided to let it go this time.

"I love you, Mom."

"I love you too, kiddo."

Darrell was surprised by how much she had

missed the sound of her mother's voice. And while she was relieved that her mother still seemed caught up in her work and happy, part of her longed just to spill everything — to tell all about her fears for Conrad and for herself going back to find him. *Oh yeah, now there's a conversation that would go well,* Darrell thought grimly. *It would convince her I'm ready for the loony bin, for sure.*

The week with Kate was seemed to last forever. Darrell had never managed to master the art of superficial polite conversation and dove into her books and research at every opportunity, much to Mrs. Clancy's chagrin. "Don't you want to go shopping, girls?" she would cry despairingly as Kate and Darrell headed back to the city library.

Darrell caught a little break one day when she and Kate met up with Brodie and Paris, taking the bus all the way out to the university to visit the acclaimed Museum of Anthropology. Completing research for Gramps made Darrell feel like she was at least making some progress in her knowledge about the Reformation. And yet, it seemed like a lesson in the intolerance of humanity throughout the eras: first against the Jewish and Muslim people during the Inquisition and then back and forth between the Protestants and the Catholics during the Reformation. Darrell recognized a discouraging pattern of ongoing dissent between three of the world's major religions; in one way or another it always seemed to be Christianity versus Judaism versus Islam.

"The Reformation is almost a bit of relief," said Brodie as they sat down to lunch at the cafeteria. "At least the Christians are going after their own for a change, instead of continually waging war on the Jewish people or the Moors."

"None of these wars were one-sided," said Kate. "The Christians weren't always wrong, either."

"You know what's interesting?" said Darrell slowly. "Everything we're learning here at the museum or in Gramps's class is already in the pages of Conrad's diary. He talks about the things he's gone through, yeah, but he also talks about the things he sees around him, day to day." She pulled the scarred old notebook out of her backpack.

"Darrell! I can't believe you are carrying that thing around with you," exclaimed Kate. "What if you lose it or something?"

Darrell smiled grimly. "I can't lose it, Kate. I think about it every waking hour." She riffled through a few pages. "Listen to this. In this bit he's talking about when he begins to help Brother Socorro get the Jews out of Spain before they are tortured or killed." She cleared her throat. "'In this age of madness, I have watched the blood flow around me like a river, watched countless pounds of human flesh seared away from bone, and I must have cried a thousand times a thousand tears. And yet, with all the agony, it still interests a part of me to note that everyone — be they Catholic Christian or heretic, Jew or Moor — everyone bleeds the same shade of red.'"

She closed the book and replaced it in her pack. "I wish I thought we had learned some of the lessons that history has to teach us," she said quietly. "but when I think of where my mom is and what she is doing, I'm not so sure."

It was a sombre group that returned on the bus that day, assignments completed. And for another of what seemed like an endless stream of nights, Darrell lay awake and worked out a plan.

Back at Eagle Glen, students threw themselves into schoolwork with new vigour. Even Paris returned with his hair a natural blonde.

"I didn't feel like colouring it, for some reason," he said sheepishly. "It still freaked my family out, though. They're convinced I'm going to move on to piercing next."

Darrell finished her watercolour of Lisbon and began one of Windsor Castle.

"You seem to have a thing for castles lately, Darrell," remarked Mr. Gill.

Gramps continued to drone on in history class, and both Paris and Brodie were slated to present their field trip project results in the first week back. The official word from Mrs. Follett was that, due to an illness at the Swiss campus, Professor Tooth was now filling in there until another teacher could be hired. And no, she didn't know when that was going to happen.

On the first Friday evening back, Darrell headed down to the beach with Delaney. They stopped for a moment at the twisted old arbutus tree behind the school and then walked down the winding path to the beach. The path was a little wider than it had been last year, cut through the pebbles and sand by the small caterpillar tractors that had ferried building materials to the site of the new coastal light.

Delaney ran ahead of Darrell, the wind ruffling his fine golden fur. She stuck her hands deep in her pockets and strolled along the edge of the shoreline. The tide was out, and seagulls wheeled and squawked their way across the sky, dive-bombing the beach with mussel shells and squabbling over tidbits.

Darrell walked out onto the point where she had first met Conrad, a day that seemed more like a decade than a year ago. Superstitiously, she craned her head over the edge, just to make sure Conrad's boat was not tucked underneath, out of sight.

Delaney barked and capered at her feet as she walked on, right up to the base of the new light. Its beacon shone out to sea day and night, oblivious to the rubble of the old lighthouse that had once stood proudly on the same spot.

With the wind at her back, Darrell walked to the other end of the beach, where giant boulders tumbled over the cliffs and down into the sea. Behind the row of boulders was the cave where Darrell's time travel adventures had begun. She stopped at the first of the giant rocks and looked back across the sand, marvelling that deep under the windswept beach a labyrinth of passages stretched into the past.

One of those passageways led directly to Conrad. She was sure of it.

Darrell lay on her bed and watched the moon rise over the mountains to the east. No lunar sliver on this cool May night. A full, round, white moon made its way across the sky while its twin swam through the water, ever westward. One o'clock was her witching hour, and by then the moon was almost ready to sink behind the mountainous islands to the west.

Delaney rose to his feet and stretched lightly before prancing out the door ahead of Darrell. They made their way down through the secret door at the back of the library and down farther still into the very bowels of the school. Darrell sat on the bottom step, the cold from the stone creeping through her jeans.

"This time we go alone, Delaney-boy. Just like the first time, remember? Except this time, let's hope we know what we're doing. The only problem we have now is — which doorway do we pick?"

The dog looked up at her, wagging his tail gently and raising his eyebrows until she smiled and made her decision. Holding his collar in one hand and her favourite walking stick in the other, she stepped toward the middle doorway as the symbol of a broken crown glowed a hot, beckoning red.

CHAPTER FIFTEEN

D arrell lay on her back, staring at the wooden beams of the ceiling for quite some time before she realized where she was. A late afternoon light poured through the window, and she saw she was in a tiny shed that held some extra benches and materials for the chapel. A knot formed in her stomach as from outside came the sound of hammering.

Darrell slipped a mint into her mouth and, after a moment or two, crept out of the shed. Delaney curled up in a sunny spot by the wall, and Darrell paused on the grass to watch as two young men constructed a high scaffold on a small paved area outside the chapel.

The Tower of London.

Darrell took a deep breath to steady her nerves. She stared around, eyes wide. There could be no doubt; it looked just like the pictures in the library books at

Eagle Glen. So she might have a chance to say goodbye to Anne, after all. With luck.

She ducked back into the side door of the chapel, needing somewhere quiet to think. The Chapel of St. Peter was quite different from the other cathedrals she had seen in this place and time. It was smaller for one, though certainly not tiny, and very old.

What had she learned of the Reformation during the time of Henry and Anne? Darrell remembered Anne reigned for barely a thousand days — as the second of Henry's wives, she had been queen for less than three years before Henry had her beheaded for treason.

Darrell shivered. The Nan she had met was full of herself and intolerant of others — especially of Katherine, Henry's first queen. But now that Darrell had entered Anne's world, she knew Anne to be a complex, fiery, flesh and blood creature. Did she have to die?

She slid onto a bench and briefly considered saying a prayer. Awkwardly, she slid off the bench onto her knees.

I don't know what to pray for. Do I pray for Anne's life? For Conrad's? I don't even know what I am praying to — how can a just God allow such terrible things to happen?

Darrell's eyes welled with tears, and she was grateful for the dim light in the tiny chapel. The cobbles dug deeply into her knees. She struggled for a few seconds to find a comfortable position but realized almost immediately that comfort was not to be found here.

She thought about the penitent she had seen on her first day in Windsor. It seemed so long ago. She remembered he had carried a scourge, or perhaps a horsewhip, and he had beaten his back with a sickeningly regular rhythm. The thin leather strap had described a lyrical arc over his head before the tip of the lash bit deeply into his own flesh. She remembered Paris's appalled face as he'd watched the man's blood trickle into his own footsteps as he walked away. That flagellant and others of his kind sought no comfort from their faith.

Darrell stood up. *I still don't know what I believe.* At the front of the chapel, a priest clad in the habit of a Grey Friar walked in the door, heavily laden with candles. Darrell slipped out the back of the chapel and into the thin sunlight of late afternoon.

A few steps from the front door a figure in a long scarlet cloak stood beside the scaffolding, perhaps watching the construction of the executioner's block. Darrell clutched her walking stick tightly and hurried nearer.

The scarlet cloak swirled in the afternoon sun, and the figure swept into the main doors of the Chapel of St. Peter. Darrell, in spite of the stiffness in the newly donned wooden leg, followed right behind.

She caught her breath for a moment in the entrance-way as her eyes adjusted to the dim light. There was no sign of the scarlet robe, but she would look all night if necessary. It had to be Conrad — it just had to be.

At the front of the chapel, the friar, dressed in a drab surplice of grey, had his back to the door, lighting candles on the altar. He moved silently in and out of the shadows. Darrell searched her memory for the name of Anne's priest.

"Excuse me," Darrell said, her voice sounding small and hollow in the open space. "Are you Father Priamos?"

The friar nodded.

"I — I wonder if you can help me. I'm looking for someone very important."

The priest hesitated a moment, and then turned to her, the heavy cowl of his robe shrouding his face.

"I am looking for — for a priest who wears a scarlet cloak," she said. "That is all I know of him, except perhaps that I think he may have white hair."

"And the name of this priest?" His voice was rough; he sounded like he needed to cough.

Darrell paused for a moment. What did she have to lose? "I know the name he was once called," she said softly. "His name was Conrad Kennedy. I don't know what his name is today, or even if he is still alive. But if he is and you know how I can find him, I beg of you to help me."

The brother pushed back the heavy cowl and exposed shiny red flesh that ran down the right side of his face like melted candle wax. He was missing an eye.

Darrell's knees failed, and she sat down hard on a low wooden bench near the altar. Could it be? But then, who was the figure in scarlet? Somehow it no longer mattered.

Unable to look at the terrible scarring, she dropped her eyes. "You have been burned," she whispered. His bark of laughter made her look into his face once again.

"Yes, Darrell Connor, I have been burned, and in more ways than one, as I am sure you will agree."

It *was* him. The room swam briefly, and she closed her eyes, head bowed like a supplicant.

After all this time. She had finally found him. She felt so guilty and wretched that all the speeches she had prepared were gone from her memory.

"I came to find you to bring you home," she said at last.

He laughed a little. "I am home," he said more gently than before. "And I did expect to see you again one day, though I knew not when."

"I'm sorry I have come so late," she whispered.

He looked at her critically. "You are just as I remember," he said, "though perhaps a little thinner and with deeper circles under your eyes. If I may ask — how much time has actually passed since the fire?"

"Almost six months."

He bowed his head and was silent for a moment.

"So little time," he said finally. "You have done well to find me after so little time. And yet look at me — I have lived a lifetime since I saw you last. Many lifetimes." He fell silent.

"Maybe — maybe you could tell me a bit about it?" Darrell ventured. "I have read the diary you left with Brother Socorro. I still have it — see?" She pulled the worn notebook out of her skirt pocket.

Friar Priamos — she still could not bear to think of him as Conrad — cleared his throat and reached over to take the small book.

"Brother Socorro was a good man," he said, his voice quaking with emotion. "I owe him my life — and much more, I owe him my spirit." He looked down at Darrell for a moment and then sat beside her on the bench. "May I keep this?" he asked.

"Of course — it's yours, after all."

"Are you sure you want to hear?" he said gently, his voice forming syllables awkwardly as he traced his way along a dialect long unspoken.

Darrell lifted her head. Her eyes burned, but she clenched her teeth and willed herself not to cry. "I need to hear," she muttered. "I need to know what I did to you."

"My child," the friar cried out, and then bit down on his words. He stared at her in silence for a moment and then laughed dryly. "It is hard to forget how close we used to be in age." He paused again. "My story is not to punish you, Darrell," he said at last. "My only wish is to set you free."

His gaze rested on her face a moment, and then he turned to look at the damp stone wall of the chapel, as if the pictures of the story he told were played out there in living colour.

"I have much to answer for," he said, his voice a mere shred above a whisper. "But that will be in another place from this one, and before a judge more terrible and beautiful than even you, my old enemy."

Darrell tried to smile. "No longer an enemy, I hope," she said.

"As do I." His voice strengthened. "I cannot think of that boy, the boy who would try to sell his friends for money, who would deliberately hurt defenceless animals, who lived in a world of betrayal — no, I cannot think of that boy as myself." His fists curled and loosened convulsively on his lap. "And yet it was from that shell of a boy I was born. Born, justly for a child begat in hell, of fire."

"I have read your journal so many times," Darrell interrupted. "It told so much, but now that I see you, I can't believe how little I know." She forced herself to look straight into his remaining eye. "How ..." Words failed her and then returned, in a rush. "How can there be so little hate? How can you not hate me?"

He paused and sighed deeply, turning his face from her. After a moment he resumed his narrative as if she hadn't spoken. "If you have read my journal, then you know most of my life as it has become. The truth is, I don't remember much of the first moments out of the flames that consumed the stable. I know I heard a gun go off — was it mine or the one held by Salvatore? I cannot remember. I just remember searing pain, and then having my arm yanked so hard I thought it would come off. My rescuer rolled me over and over on the ground outside the burning stable, though I'm not sure if my clothes were aflame or simply smoking. My legs and torso bear no scars from the fire, so I have to think he rolled me out of instinct more than any altruistic need to save my life. In fact, he took one look at me and vomited into the ditch.

"I lay on the ground where he'd left me, the hard rime of frost biting into the rawness that once had been my face."

Darrell flinched but clenched her hands together tightly, unable to take her eyes from Conrad's face.

"I just lay there and listened to the closest thing I had to friends scream as the fire consumed them. I closed my eyes and waited for the end to come. The man who had pulled me to safety had shown no mercy. It seems that the sight of me and the blackened charcoal that passed for my skin was too much for him.

After spilling his guts on the street he got to his feet and I never saw him again."

The old friar shivered a little. He stood suddenly and poured a splash of wine from a jug on the altar into a ceramic cup and leaned forward to sip from it.

"Medicinal," he said, and the right side of his face quirked into a smile. He sat down again. "The screaming didn't last, of course. That old stable was filled with straw and debris and was built of powdery old wooden beams. It went up like a roman candle, and the roar of the flames soon drowned any other sound."

Darrell put a hand on his arm. "You thought we might have burned to death? And we thought the same of you." She shook her head sadly. "All of us wrong."

He nodded his agreement. "The night, or rather early morning as it now had become, was cold, but the crisp air and frozen ground couldn't hold the flames back. The dry cold of that February morning in Firenze kept all decent citizens wrapped up tightly in their beds and asleep past the time when the smell of smoke might have saved the stable.

"By the time a call rang through the streets, the stable was no longer the issue. The stable, in fact, was no longer there. I watched as the tiny sparks that kaleidoscoped skyward in blue and green and vivid orange-red danced across the lane to the thatched roof of a neighbouring potting shed. Tongues of flame licked the walls of the nearby house, slipping through cracks and sliding along crevices to the wooden beams inside the mud- and clay-covered walls.

"I could only watch the fire move with one eye, for I knew the other eye to be full of mud. I lay there and wait- ed for the wind to turn. The merest hint of a breeze would bring the flames back to my spot on the frozen, rutted mud track, and I would be engulfed. The bells that signalled the gates of hell had truly opened began to toll, one after the other, summoning all lost souls. I closed my eyes to the brilliant sight and waited for death.

"It was the mud that saved me, you know. The frozen road where I waited for death slowly thawed in the heat from the flames. The thick muck, churned into ridges and tracks by the hooves of many horses and the wheels of many carts, softened and plastered itself in a thick mass to one side of my face. The occupants of the house next to Verocchio's old ruin discovered the flames too late to save their own home but early enough to save all the family members and to peel my remains off the ground. By my very strangeness, they must sure- ly have believed me to be the source of this flaming tragedy. The two youngest sons, stalwart lads in their early twenties, scraped me up and flung me without cer- emony into the back of a cart with the few belongings they were able to salvage before their villa burned to the ground. A donkey was hastily hitched to the cart and, led by the lady of the house, trundled to the only place of sanctuary the local residents could imagine: the Church of Saint Mary de Fiores, The Duomo."

A quiet knock at the door made Darrell jump as though she had been struck.

"Father? The lady awaits you."

The friar gathered his cloak closely around his shoulders and pulled the cowl back up to shroud his face.

He turned to Darrell and took her hands in his own. "That is more than enough," he said, his voice steady. "My first duty now is to my lady in this hour of her most desperate need. All that remains is for me to ask your forgiveness."

"My forgiveness?" she choked. "I am here to seek your forgiveness — for leaving you behind in time, for consigning you to a life — in hell."

"For *sparing* me a life in hell," he said gently. "Think well on this, Darrell Connor. You did not condemn me anywhere. I chose to make my own decisions, right or wrong. And here I have found a life that has meaning for me."

She shook her head. "I can't believe the Conrad Kennedy I knew would ever want to be a priest."

He gave his strange half-smile. "The Conrad Kennedy you knew no longer exists. He was lost that day in a terrible fire. But the man that was reborn out of that shell of a boy is able to give some comfort to others. Nearby, a woman will walk to her own death at the hands of her husband, perhaps as soon as tomorrow, and I hope to offer her some comfort."

"But — does your religion give *you* any comfort?"

His eye gleamed in the candle light. "The truth is, I've come to look at organized religion as the source of many of the world's problems, rather than a cure for them," he said quietly. "However, I do think everyone has the right to worship in whatever way suits them best."

"I can't believe that's a very popular viewpoint these days," said Darrell wryly.

"You're absolutely correct," said Conrad. "And so I wear the habit and follow the rules of the Franciscan order, but like Socorro, I help things along — in my own way."

He walked over to the door. "Perhaps we shall meet again," he said.

"Tomorrow?"

"Perhaps." The door closed gently, and Darrell was left alone with her long-ago thoughts. She collected her stick and walked slowly out of the chapel.

Conrad, found at last — and almost unrecognizable in the end. Darrell paused with her hand on the doorway. But if Conrad was a Grey Friar, then who had been watching her all this time, wearing the scarlet cloak?

Chapter Sixteen

She stepped outside the chapel, and Delaney ran up to greet her. Darrell reached down to pat him, more as a comfort to herself than to him, when she heard her name being called.

"Mistress Dara! Oh, can it really be you?" To her surprise, Lady Jacqueline, whom she remembered as one of Katherine of Aragon's personal attendants, was scurrying across the grass. She scattered a group of three ravens as she ran, and they marched out of her way like shiny black soldiers, unable to fly on their clipped wings.

Jacqueline grasped Darrell delightedly by both shoulders and spoke with her strong French accent. "The queen told me she had seen you through the window of her room, and indeed she was quite correct. She will be simply delighted you are here, on this of all days."

"I — I have come a long way to see her, Lady Jacqueline. But ..." Darrell hesitated. How to say it? "Is she all right?" She kicked herself mentally. What kind of stupid question was that? How could the queen be all right? She was facing her own execution.

Lady Jacqueline smiled. "She is well enough at the moment," she replied. "She has often been unwell, these past few months, but now she is calm and prepared."

"Even with a full view of this — this thing?" Darrell pointed to the executioner's block.

"Even with that. She had just called for her confessor the moment she saw you, so will tarry but a moment with him, I am sure. She is most anxious to see you. Please follow me."

Darrell trailed behind Lady Jacqueline, leaving Delaney curled up in his sunny spot outside. "This is the Queen's House," said Jacqueline. "Henry had it built here within the Tower especially for Anne, poor thing — before she lost the wee boy."

The house was the only building of its kind on the Tower grounds, and Jacqueline led Darrell past a collection of meeting and private rooms, all beautifully appointed. As they entered the personal chamber of the queen, a chorus of mourning arose from Anne's ladies. They were sitting by the window, watching the progress of the building of the executioner's block.

"She is dead, dead," lamented one, Lady Rachel.

"Dead to us all," wailed another.

"It is her own witchery to blame," whispered the third.

"Nonsense," snapped Jacqueline, with a glance at Darrell's stricken face. "Lady Rachel, you know Queen Anne is no more a witch than I am."

The three ladies shuffled away from Jacqueline, eyeing her warily.

"Your hair *is* red," hissed Rachel.

"As is the king's," said Jacqueline, exasperated. "Or it was before it started to thin out and turn grey."

"Anne's hair is dark," whispered Darrell, able to speak at last. The nattering of the women left her feeling sick and useless. What good was it to travel through time when there was no way to help those in need?

"Black as her eyes, black as her soul," sang Lady Rachel.

Darrell stepped forward, her hands balled into tight fists at her side. "You are her ladies," she said incredulously. "Is it not your place to support your queen?"

Jacqueline turned her back on the others, and Darrell could see her eyes were shiny with unshed tears. She collected her embroidery from a basket by the window. "I am loyal to my queen," she whispered quietly, "for I have been with her since she returned to this country from the court of Queen Claude in France."

"That could be to your peril," said Rachel and arched an eyebrow at Darrell. "Our first loyalty is to the king and to God," she said. She pulled a small package from a hidden pocket inside her voluminous skirts and carefully unwrapped an ornate pen from its protective roll of cotton.

"This pen was given me by the king himself," she said proudly. "He bade us record every word the witch utters, for evidence at her trial, is this not so, Gwendolyn?"

"Her ravings have been as of a madwoman," agreed Lady Gwendolyn, smoothing her skirts. "One moment laughing, the next she is on her knees bewailing her fate."

Darrell turned on her furiously. "In her place, how would you feel? Not sure if you would live or die, your fate imposed upon you by the man you love?"

"Perhaps," said Rachel, batting her eyelashes knowingly. "And perhaps she loves another. At least one of her lovers awaits his fate in the Tower."

Darrell sat weakly down on a cushioned window seat. The words of Anne's ladies sounded like so much chattering of blackbirds. "What is she supposed to have done?" she asked despairingly. "I know he says she is an enchantress who bewitched him away from Queen Katherine. But is that enough to have her executed?"

"My lady the queen is accused of plotting treason against the the kingdom of Britain and its monarch," whispered Jacqueline.

"She is a traitor in more ways than one," crowed Gwendolyn. "She is accused of adultery and of plotting against the king, her fine husband."

"If Elizabeth had been born a boy, Anne would have been untouchable," hissed Jacqueline. "Queen Anne has always spoken her mind clearly, and Henry has tired of her as he did of Katherine when she was unable to produce a male heir." She wrung her handkerchief in her hands. "If only she would hold her tongue rather than always speaking her mind! The king looks now to the modest and quiet Lady Jane Seymour instead of his beautiful Anne."

"Is there no one who will speak to her innocence?" asked Darrell.

"The queen herself confesses to nothing, beyond humbling herself before God and the king," insisted Lady Jacqueline.

"And what of her supposed suitors?" asked Darrell.

"Smeaton," breathed Rachel, and the ladies all sighed, a sound so synchronized it might have been rehearsed.

"So handsome — such a waste," said Lady Gwendolyn, and Darrell could hear a catch in her voice that wasn't present when she spoke of her doomed queen.

"A true gentleman of the court, Mark Smeaton," continued Lady Rachel. Her voice dropped to a whisper. "The king has declined him mercy, and on the morrow he is to endure the most grievous pain of death the courts can impart."

Lady Jacqueline jumped to her feet and burst into tears. "Speak of it no more," she cried. "For think upon this. If these honoured members of the court are so treated when unjustly accused, what of ourselves? What shall be our fate?" Clutching her handkerchief, she stumbled through the door.

Darrell stood up to follow Jacqueline and glanced over at the remaining ladies-in-waiting. Gwendolyn's skin had gone very pale, though Rachel shot Darrell a venomous glance.

"Anne is not a witch," Darrell repeated. "And she is the mother of a little girl. This is not justice." She stepped out to find Jacqueline standing in the hall, her composure somewhat restored.

Lady Jacqueline bowed her head. "The king has kept the queen away from her daughter, but these last seventeen days Anne has been allowed to spend time with Elizabeth. The queen has now left her confessor and will spend a few moments with her daughter at present. Would you join them?"

Darrell nodded and glanced back into the room to see Rachel furiously scribbling on a long roll of paper.

"I simply could not believe my eyes when I spied you coming out of the chapel," Anne said, smiling gently. "I am more delighted to see your face than you can possibly know."

Darrell nodded dumbly as Anne waved Lady Jacqueline out of the room. She clutched her stick and walked over to where Anne was sitting with a sleeping child in her arms. The tiny princess's face was serene, and Anne clutched her protectively. An old brass pendulum swung to and fro, dully reflecting the firelight across the toddler's round, sleeping face.

Anne placed the child in a raised trundle bed and leaned wearily on the corner of small wooden frame. "Hard to countenance that until an hour past she was still running and making merry," she whispered.

"Are you tired, milady?" Darrell placed her walking stick in the corner near the door and sat on a stool next to the fire.

"I *am* tired." Anne smiled and tucked a strand of fine red hair into place on the sleeping girl's head. "But I enjoy the child's company, while I have her." She quietly lifted a hard wooden chair from near the window and sat down beside Darrell, and her voice dropped. "Sitting here, I am loath to believe this beauty's father has vowed to put her mother to death."

Darrell reached over to squeeze Anne's hand.

"Perhaps he'll change his mind. Could he not grant you a divorce?"

Anne shrugged, but her smile was sad. She stood and drew a curtain across the alcove where Elizabeth slept and then returned to sit with Darrell.

"I knew you'd be back — he told me he thought you would."

"Who told you?"

"Priamos, of course. I spend most of my time with him, these days."

"But when I last saw you, you told me Friar Priamos was leaving."

"He did leave — for a while. But after Elizabeth's birth, he returned. He said he thought I might need some comfort, and indeed, he was correct." Anne touched Darrell's shoulder. "I am ready, you know. Whether it be tomorrow or next week, I know my heart is true to my sovereign and to my God." She looked at Darrell with the large, dark eyes that had beguiled one of the most powerful rulers of all time. "I am not a witch," she whispered.

Darrell swallowed hard. "I know that, your Majesty. I just wish you could convince the king."

Anne shook her head. "That is immaterial now. He believes me a traitor and a witch, therefore it is true. My only hope now is for my daughter, that she be given her rightful due as heir to the throne. I fear for her now ..." Anne bowed her head, unable to continue.

Darrell bit her lip. What to say to comfort a woman who would surely be dead within days? "Your daughter has the same fire in her eyes that you carry, your Majesty," she whispered. "You must not fear. Have ..." Darrell stopped herself short. How could she counsel this queen to have something she could not find in her own heart — faith? "Have strength, your Majesty," she finished lamely.

Anne stood up and strode across to the window. Darrell watched her look out upon the afternoon, sunny and fine. Workers scurried to and fro across the courtyard, erecting poles for banners and string lines that would be used to hang bunting and other colourful indications of her own death.

"It is hard to feel a part of the world anymore," she said quietly. "Soon the country will celebrate the death of the Great Enemy. The witch." She turned from the window and looked at Darrell. "And yet, here I am. I am still of the world. I eat. I long for my child and for those few years of happiness I shared with my husband." She laughed a little. "I sleep — I dream. Dara, I dreamed of you last night. It is how I knew you would arrive to be with me today."

She swept over to sit beside Darrell, her black skirts and crinolines rustling as she primly tucked them into place. She looked down at her hands and impatiently began to undo the fine buttons on the lace gloves she was rarely seen without. She tossed the gloves on the floor.

"Yet another pretence cast aside," she said disdainfully. She lay her long hands on her lap, the small protrusion on the side of her right finger hardly noticeable in the dark room. "Sign of the witch, this thing." She laughed again and patted Darrell's leg. "I am no more a witch than you, Dara."

She was quiet a moment, staring into space. A smile fluttered around her lips. "You were flying, in my dream, Dara. On the back of some strange beast — surely not akin to any horse I have ever seen. And on the back of this beast, I could see where you clung to an apparition."

Darrell's stomach contracted in a knot and she clenched her hands in her lap. This was not supposed to happen. She was here to say goodbye — not to hear portents that hovered too close to the truth from a woman too close to death. Anne took Darrell's hands in her own.

"I thought the apparition at first to be death — my own death, riding on a black horse, with you clinging on behind. But no — in this dream, death was seeking you, Dara, not I."

Darrell swallowed. Her mouth felt strangely dry. "It was only a dream, your Majesty," she said quietly. "Think of it no more."

"No — no. I must tell you. A strange piece of black helm covered your head and masked your eyes, yet I knew it was you. You were little more than a baby, perhaps nine or ten years old. The apparition I thought was death turned out to be an angel — a dark angel, but one who would deliver you from the long, dark sleep."

The sounds of the workers outside seemed to fade into the distance as the doomed queen spoke. Darrell felt herself drawn into Anne's words, images that could have been pulled from the shreds of her own memory.

"When death appeared, all I could see were the impossibly round, yellow eyes as it advanced, unblinking, upon you. I knew you would be swallowed alive and I cried out, but of course, no sound could I make for it was a dream. The strange steed you rode veered to one side, and I could see the knight who rode with you wrestling for control. And — it was as though time stood still."

Darrell sat as if paralyzed. How could Anne know these things? She felt as though she were drowning in the dark pools of Anne's eyes.

"He bore no weapon against the great monster death, your knight," Anne continued, speaking as though still deep in the dream. "But in that last instant before it sprang, his strength was greater than that of a thousand men and he needed no weapon. With a single arm he swept you up and hurled you away from the path of the monster."

Anne dropped her head, her voice muffled. "And then death took him, and I knew it as I awoke."

Darrell's vision fogged and she struggled to stay conscious. "The accident," she whispered. "How could you know, your Majesty?"

Darrell looked past the queen and stared blindly out the window at the workers as they readied the block for Anne's dance with death below. And remembered …

She had awakened in the dark, with something wet running down her face. There was no pain, at first. It was more like a gradual widening of her mind followed by a critical assessment of her body. Her first view was of the sky, the stars reflecting dimly in the water of the Sound.

Sky. Stars. Not rain on her face then. Her neck was stretched back, her head draped downwards. For a moment, the beauty of the night took her breath away, borne on a fragrance of broken pine boughs. Too beautiful to be real — perhaps it was just a dream? She lay without motion, gazing at the inverted night world of wood and water. How much more beautiful it would be the right way around — she should sit up. With her first movement, though, came sure, black knowledge. All was not well. Perhaps there would, in fact, never be beauty again. She couldn't lift her head, so instead struggled to roll onto her side.

The bolt of pain that shot up her leg was singular in its intensity and mercifully brief in duration. She leaned forward and gazed at her leg in disbelief. Her foot lay unresponsive on the asphalt road. And where was her shoe? As she watched, a pool of blood erupted from the cuff of her pant leg, smothering the brown skin. The dark blood puddled and flowed away across the black asphalt, and the jagged bone protruding where her ankle had been was stark in the starlight. Her breath caught in her throat, and she leaned weakly to the other side, supported on her arm, and vomited. This provided no relief from the pain, but it surely meant her dad would come. She never had to be sick alone.

"Daddy?" Her voice wouldn't work — so maybe it was a dream after all. "Dad?"

And in the way of dreams, her dad couldn't hear her, for he was gone. "I'll just wait here, Daddy," she whispered. "You'll come — it's getting a little foggy, you just need time to find me."

And waiting for her father, Darrell passed out on the pine bracken that had, moments before, saved her life.

Tears running freely down her face, Darrell turned back to the doomed queen. "I never got to say goodbye to him," she said, her voice barely audible.

245

"Perhaps not," responded the queen, and she placed her hand warmly on Darrell's arm. "But he bade his farewell to you, for as the monster took him, I saw him smile."

Darrell nodded and sat silent for a long moment. "Thank you," she said at last, feeling the tears still wet on her cheeks. "Your dream has let me see the truth. I see now that I did not really need to say goodbye to my father. He is always with me — he is in my memories and in my heart."

"And on your lips — for your smile is as like his as my girl's is like Henry's," said Anne softly.

Darrell wiped her face on the lace handkerchief that Anne held out to her and smiled wryly. "This is not as it should be. I am here to offer you solace and instead you have done so for me. I so wish that I could be of further help to you, your Majesty."

Anne smiled at her. "My tears are done — all the screaming and denying is over. My heart is at peace, Dara. And if my dream has brought you comfort, then I am the happier for it."

Darrell smoothed down her heavy skirts, feeling as though a huge burden had lifted from her heart. What could she do in return? She cleared her throat and watched Anne carefully as she spoke.

"You said earlier that you are no more a witch than I, and I know that to be true. But I also know you saw us take our leave in Windsor forest. I hope you understand that we are not witches or supernatural — but we are not of this time."

"I cannot deny that your stange disappearance that day in the forest ensured my reputation as a witch with Lady Margaret, to be sure."

Darrell twisted the handkerchief in her hands, but as Anne's face showed only calm, she decided to risk a little more.

"Please hold in your heart the knowledge of this truth. Your daughter will prosper and receive her due as heir to her father's throne. Though you have not borne Henry a son, know that your greatest hope will come true. Elizabeth will reign strong and sure. Her legacy will outlast all others of her era and her name will be revered for centuries."

A trumpet sounded outside and Anne bowed her head. "I know not how you see these things," she said quietly. "Perhaps your dreams are as vivid as my own. But I thank you, for you have brought my heart peace." She swept to the window. "And now you must go," she said, and her voice was no longer that of a frightened woman, but resounded with the will of the Queen of England. "The trumpet sounds to call the court once more into session and I to my fate."

She leaned in from the window. "I think perhaps you may want to make your way to the chapel once more,

Dara. It is there that my own confessor, Friar Priamos, readies my soul for its journey. It is there, as with all good places, that you shall find your sanctuary."

The door to the chamber flung open so rapidly that it bounced against the wall. One of the king's men stepped across the threshold and took hold of Anne's arm.

"You are to come with me, witch."

"There is no need to be rough, good sir. I will do as you say."

The guard pulled the queen to the door of her chamber. "If you believe me to be a witch," Anne remarked dryly, "you might take care that I do not think to curse you for your lack of gentleness."

The guard looked so startled he actually dropped her arm for a moment. She gave a final smile to Darrell. "Stay safe, young woman," she said. "I will remember you in my prayers." She turned to the guard. "Let us proceed," she said, and with a much gentler hand, he guided her out of sight.

CHAPTER SEVENTEEN

Darrell stumbled outside to find Delaney sitting with a companion. Lady Jacqueline turned a tear-stained face to the sun.

"We but await the final announcement of her execution date."

Darrell hoisted her heavy skirts in one arm and reached down to help Jacqueline up from where she had been seated beside Delaney. "Watching this whole thing unfold is sickening. I feel completely helpless."

"As do I." Jacqueline tucked one arm into Darrell's. "Do you mind if we walk? I have news that I would share with you," she said, keeping her voice low.

"That would be wonderful," said Darrell with a sigh. "I could use some good news right about now." She stood still a moment. "It doesn't by chance have anything to do with a priest in a scarlet robe?"

Jacqueline looked puzzled. "Perhaps you mean one of the cardinals? No, my news has nothing to do with the church, except most indirectly." She sighed. "You must be strong, Mistress Dara. The young lad from the stable has just called out that the conspirators in the Tower have been summarily executed. Anne's brother and the three other men were killed at dawn."

Darrell blanched. "And that is supposed to be *good* news?"

Jacqueline shook her head. "The only good part is that the king showed his mercy at the last. They were sentenced for treason, which can mean they were to be drawn and quartered before being burned at the stake. The poor men were to be hung high by their necks and cut down before death. Following this they were to be disembowelled while still alive and then cut into pieces before burning — the most grievous punishment the law can mete out. But Henry stepped in and commuted their sentences, so instead of the terrible deaths, they were swiftly beheaded."

Darrell swayed a little and sat down on a hay bale. "I saw Mark Smeaton in the dining hall once," she whispered. "And now he has had his head cut off?" Her hand rose to her own throat.

"This is not news," she muttered under her breath. "I knew this was going to happen, I read about it in the library." She stood with Jacqueline's helping hand. "It is hard to believe that cutting someone's head off can be considered merciful."

The door swung open, and a young stable boy careened into the stall. He nodded at Jacqueline. "Lady Jacqueline, ma'am, Lady Rachel is looking for you and the other miss."

Jacqueline squatted down on the straw-covered floor in front of the boy. "Did she say why, Byron?"

He shook his head and wiped the back of his hand across his face. "No, miss. She was standing with that priest and with milord Norfolk. She smiled at me and sent me to fetch you to the court."

"Did the priest have a scarlet hood, Byron?" asked Darrell urgently.

The boy nodded.

"The court!" Jacqueline looked at Darrell, the colour draining out of her face. She grabbed the stable boy by the shoulders and shook him a little. "Did Lord Norfolk say anything?" she demanded.

The boy grimaced and tried to wriggle out of her grasp. "I heard but a scrap," he said. "The lady said you were the queen's women and Lord Norfolk said that your fates should be as hers." He struggled against Jacqueline's grip. " Lerroff!" he shouted. "That be all I know!" With a final violent twist he spun out of her grasp and disappeared out the stable door.

"Our fate shall be as hers?" said Darrell slowly.

They looked at each other in dismay. "What shall we do, Dara?" said Jacqueline, her face white to the lips.

"You must leave now," said Darrell urgently. "We have run out of time if Norfolk has his eye on us. I have read of this man — he will do anything to save his own skin. He's Anne's uncle but also her judge. Norfolk has sent his own nephew to his death, and his niece will likely be next."

Jacqueline's hands trembled. "My brother told me it might come to this," she said. She reached out and took Darrell's hands into her own. "Come with me," she pleaded. "My brother crossed the sea with me many years ago when I came with the queen, and he works as a smith in London. He will find us safe passage back to France."

"But how can we get out of the Tower without anyone seeing us?" said Darrell.

Jacqueline strode to the door of the stable. "We shall make our way out the way my poor queen arrived — through Traitor's Gate."

"But that is a gate to the Thames," whispered Darrell. "How can you make it through the water?"

Jacqueline drew a small velvet bag from within her skirts. "I keep my jewels and a few pieces of gold with me always — they will pay our way," she said. "The gateman will turn his eye away from me, with enough persuasion." She shook the small bag, and its contents rattled gently. "My brother's smithy is just across the

Thames. We need only to swim under the wharf — a matter of a few feet. It is near darkness now — we must leave at once. It is our only hope."

Darrell smiled grimly.

"Then you must take it. But I will not come with you."

"But, Dara, if you do not escape with me, Norfolk will have you to the block with Queen Anne!" She glanced down at Darrell's walking stick. "Do not fear your crippled foot will slow me down, dear lady — I have seen how well you manage. You must take off the wooden peg for the river, of course, but my brother will surely make you a crutch or even a new peg when he hears of our plight."

Darrell peered out the door of the stable and stilled Jacqueline's outburst with a raised hand. "You must go at once," she said urgently. "Norfolk has just emerged from the Garden Tower and crosses the Green. You have a workable plan, my lady, but I'm afraid I cannot go with you."

Jacqueline paled. "But you will surely die with our beloved queen." She drew herself up. "Perhaps I should do the same. It is only right that I stay in service to my lady to the end, no matter how bitter it may be."

"Nonsense." Darrell tried not to let her alarm show. "Think of your brother, Jacqueline, and your family in France. Besides," she said, smiling a little, "I have no intention of letting Norfolk separate me from my head. You must trust that I have another way out of the Tower, dear lady. You did not see me enter, remember? I will leave as I arrived and will stay safe, I promise. Now please see to your own safety. Run!"

After shooing the still-weeping Jacqueline out the rear stable door, Darrell dashed back to the window. Norfolk had vanished from sight, but behind the newly erected executioner's block, she confirmed what she had seen but not told Jacqueline: a swirl of scarlet robe.

Delaney at her heels, she hurried as fast as the awkward wooden foot would allow across the open Green towards the Chapel of St. Peter. She had just reached the site of the scaffold when a hand shot out from behind the wooden framework and clutched her arm in its iron grip.

Delaney growled at the liveried soldier who held Darrell pinned tightly in his grasp. The soldier swung a heavily booted foot at the dog, and Delaney backed away a few feet, his teeth bared.

"One of the queen's ladies, is it not?" The oily tones of a voice that could only belong to Norfolk whispered out of the shadows. The duke stepped forward into the setting rays of the sun. "To where do you hurry on this clear spring evening? Shouldn't you be with your queen at the occasion of her final sunset?"

Darrell wrenched her arm out of the soldier's grip. "How can you speak that way? Anne is your own niece — your brother's daughter. Have you no pity for her?"

The duke laughed. "My dear niece has outlasted her usefulness. You may be interested to know that just moments ago she was condemned to death. On the morrow, her head will rest easy on a soft cushion, courtesy of a fine swordsman's blade." He smiled. "In her extremity, it is my fondest wish that her loyal ladies accompany Anne on her final journey."

Darrell glanced over the duke's shoulder, judging the distance she would have to sprint to reach the small shed behind the chapel. The distance seemed impossibly large — not exactly the convenient escape route she had described to Jacqueline. And where was Delaney?

"I — I am but a visitor to the queen on her final day," she said, stalling. Where had the dog gone? "Anne's ladies are loyal first to King Henry — surely you know that, your Grace? They carefully copy her every word for use at the trial."

"It was I who presided at her final trial, goose," he spat. "'Twas I who read the words written by her ladies. But it is not of those ladies I speak. The Frenchwoman — Jacqueline is her name? Originally from that harridan Claude's court, if I am not mistaken. Yes, I do believe that Anne should have company on her final walk, and you two ladies, true to the last, should meet your ends with the fallen witch. Take away this slime," he snarled. "And I've seen the other one making eyes at the guard at Traitor's Gate. Ensure you take both the woman and the guard to meet their just ends."

The soldier's glove closed around Darrell's shoulder once more, and the walking stick was wrenched from her hand. Panic rose in her throat. Delaney? She struggled against the soldier, landing a decent kick to his shin with her wooden foot. He reached around and lifted her bodily off the ground.

As soon as he could see Darrell was no longer a threat, the Duke of Norfolk stepped close to the soldier. "Take her to the Garden Tower," he hissed. "And she may await the morrow with the French woman and her gate guard."

"A word in your ear, your Grace." A quiet, somehow familiar voice carried over the sound of Darrell's struggle with the guard. She looked over and gaped. The scarlet-cloaked figure stood in the shadows of the wooden scaffolding, the wagging tail of a dog just visible behind the heavy woollen robes.

The last ray of the setting sun glanced off a weighty gold chain around the priest's surplice, and Darrell found herself temporarily blinded by the searing glare.

"Allow me to take your prisoner for a final word of comfort. You have my word that she will meet due justice."

Norfolk spluttered a little. "But *Monsignore* — you would not deny this supporter of the traitor queen her just reward?"

"Not at all." The voice was calm and very cool to the duke. "No more than you would question my authority to give this poor soul her last rites?"

The duke shrugged, acquiescing with thinly disguised disgust. "If I have your word, *Monsignore*, then I know it is as if I had the word of Rome. Take her away. I trust you know your way to the Garden Tower?"

The red hood nodded curtly and leaned toward the duke. "A bloody final waiting place, indeed," the priest said in a low voice and put a gentle hand on Darrell's arm. With the glare of the sun still in her eyes, Darrell snatched her walking stick from the guard's glove and hurried after the scarlet robe as it swept in through the side door of the Chapel of St. Peter.

Dashing into the chapel door, Darrell ran straight into the arms of Friar Priamos. Darrell rubbed her eyes, trying hard to adjust to the near darkness inside.

"To the shed at the back," he said. "There is no time to waste. Norfolk will soon see through the ruse when he finds the *Monsignore* has actually been with Henry all this time."

"What …?" Darrell couldn't find the words to put to the dozen or so questions that bubbled all at once into her brain.

"No time," the man who had once been Conrad Kennedy repeated. He hustled her into the tiny shed behind the chapel. "Be safe, Darrell — and Delaney." Priamos reached down, and though Delaney ducked his head a little, he stood bravely in place as the priest patted a final goodbye.

Darrell stepped through the doorway of the shed. "I am Dara," she said to the figure inside.

"Yes," came the response in a familiar voice, "though I know you better by another name."

Darrell's jaw dropped as she found herself gazing into the deep green eyes of Professor Myrtle Tooth.

Grasping her dog tightly by the old knotted rope around his neck, she took the hand of the scarlet figure, and together they stepped under the doorframe that bore the burning symbol of a dying falcon.

Chapter Eighteen

Darrell sat on the bottom of the stone steps leading up to the school library. She swirled a mint in her mouth and, after a moment, remembered to offer one to her travelling companion.

"I thought you were Conrad," she said quietly.

Professor Tooth nodded. "He told me so. I have a certain fondness for that scarlet robe, you know. Buried in its folds I can pass almost anywhere *Anno Domini*. But perhaps I need to take off a few pounds. It is remarkable how often I am mistaken for a male member of the clergy."

Darrell noticed with a grin that her teacher pocketed the mint. "Mistaken? Professor Tooth, you can't fool me — you deliberately disguised yourself."

"But in fact, I *could* fool you — and did, as I recall." The school principal dusted off the sensible wool skirt she now wore. "As you well know, Darrell, the cultural mores of the sixteenth century do not reflect any sort of equality between women and men. If I must make my way through the centuries dressed as a male, so be it."

Darrell nodded. "I have been trying to find you all term, Professor. Have you been with Conrad the whole time?"

Professor Tooth smiled a little. "I have been back and forth, my dear. A school principal has many things to attend to these days, but my students' welfare takes absolute precedence."

"So — you weren't in Switzerland after all?"

"I believe I made a little side-trip there near the beginning of the term. Let's just say it is a convenient spot from which to make a telephone call."

Darrell leaned against the rocky wall. "I was so angry that you weren't watching out for Conrad, but you had your eye on him all the time."

"I have many students to care about, my dear, including yourself."

Darrell ducked her head away from the piercing intelligence that shone from her principal's green eyes. "Thank you for coming to help me," she said quietly, head bowed.

"I didn't give you any help, Darrell. You found the answers you sought all by yourself. It just struck me that you might like a little company on your journey home."

Professor Tooth consulted her wristwatch. "And now, I believe it is time we made our way up to the library. I have sent word for a small meeting of sorts, and it is due to begin very shortly."

Delaney wiggled his way past Darrell on the tightly winding steps and padded up alongside Professor Tooth.

Darrell could hear the teacher's quiet voice echoing down the stairwell. "Lovely to see you again, Delaney. Lovely to be back, in fact. I have so missed this place."

The secret door into the library was still slightly ajar, and as Darrell walked through she collected the book she had used as a prop to return to the shelves.

Professor Tooth reached out a hand. "May I?"

Darrell handed the book to the principal and glanced at the cover herself for the first time. "*The Six Wives of Henry VIII*," read Professor Tooth. "An apt choice, my dear."

The door to the library burst open, and Kate came charging into the room, followed closely by Paris and Brodie. Her mouth dropped open at the sight of the school principal.

"Miss Clancy! My goodness, that is no way to make your way through the halls of Eagle …" Mrs. Follett stopped chastising Kate mid-stream as she spotted the school principal from where she stood near the door. "Why Professor Tooth! Where did you come from? And when did you arrive back from Europe? Oh my, I just feel terrible to not have been at the front door to meet your taxi. Such a long drive from the airport, too! I do believe —"

"Not to worry, Mrs. Follett," Professor Tooth interrupted smoothly. "It was far too early an hour for me to expect anyone to meet me. And I am afraid it is my fault these students are careening through the school. I had just sent a very urgent message for them to join me here in the library."

"Oh my goodness, Professor, I do hope everything is all right?"

"Of course, Mrs. Follett, everything is just fine. I am quite delighted to be back at school, I must say, though the term is nearly over and I seem to have missed a great number of goings-on."

"Indeed you have, Professor Tooth. Why just the other day —"

"Mrs. Follett, I'm terribly sorry to cut you off, but would you mind dreadfully if I ask you to gather together all the papers that require my signature? I am sure there are several important issues that cry out for my immediate attention. I will meet you down in my office very shortly."

"Of course, Professor." Mrs. Follett scurried away, her head filled with happy visions of papers filed carefully away. The school principal turned once more to her students.

She smiled warmly at the group, all of whom looked more than a little shell-shocked by the latest turn of events.

"Perhaps we might sit a moment?" she asked politely. As the students pulled chairs around the small table near the back of the library, Professor Tooth smiled again. "I have much that demands my attention downstairs, as I am sure you know," she said, "but I feel somehow that you may have a question or two that I might be able to address briefly."

While the others stared at one another in stunned silence, Darrell laughed.

"A question or two?" she said. "Try a thousand. I don't even know where to begin. Professor Tooth, I have been wanting to talk to you since the first day of the term."

"Since I do not have time to answer a thousand questions, perhaps you might begin with one you had on that first day of school," replied the principal.

Darrell thought for a moment. "I guess I know part of the answer now," she said slowly, "but when school started I was really angry. I was angry at myself for somehow allowing Conrad to travel through time with us. I felt responsible for losing him — and I thought he was dead, so I felt that was my fault, too. But I was also angry with you, Professor. I mean, you're the principal of our school, however odd a place it may be. And therefore you have ultimate responsibility. How can you call yourself the principal and not be there to take care of the students?" Darrell looked around the table at her friends. "We all know so much more than when we came to this school," she continued. "I don't think you'd get any argument from us that this place is the most amazing school in the world. But the risks of time travel are so enormous ... How can you let us take those risks unsupervised?"

Professor Tooth was silent a moment, her strong fingers interlocked on the table.

"You ask a complex and intelligent question, Darrell," she said at last. "But the truth is that every teacher exposes his or her students to risk with each new piece of knowledge they impart. You may well ask how any teacher can let students go anywhere near a world loaded with danger that can take the form of everything from physical risk to drugs and exploitation to emotional turmoil. This is a concern teachers and parents face every day."

The principal got to her feet. "When I signed on as a teacher, I had to accept that there is a real world out there, and that it is my responsibility to introduce the children in my care to the information that will help them make the right choices."

She walked around the table and put a hand on Darrell's shoulder. "I know you have been angry at me this term, Darrell. I regret most that you have felt deserted, because that is a feeling with which you are all too achingly familiar. And yet, I do not believe that anger is necessarily always a bad thing. Sometimes it can be a motivator, pushing people to make changes and learn more."

The principal looked around the table. "I believe I am correct in guessing that there is much more all of you care to learn." Every head nodded.

Professor Myrtle Tooth smiled. "Then perhaps you should count yourselves lucky that you enrolled at this particular school," she said. "We specialize in learning new things, here at Eagle Glen."

She turned to leave. "And now I am afraid I must go address Mrs. Follett's paperwork backlog," she said. "You'll be happy to know that Professor Grampian has agreed to stay on to finish the term. I'm sure Mrs. Follett has more than enough work to keep me busy until them."

The door closed almost silently behind the departing principal. "I feel like I've been hit by a two-tonne bag of feathers," said Darrell. "Pretty soft blow, but two tonnes is two tonnes, after all."

"I'm just so glad you're okay," said Kate. "I woke up at three this morning, and when I saw your empty bed I knew right away that you'd gone into the past alone again. I've been so worried all morning. I guess you didn't — you didn't find Conrad after all."

Darrell stood up, relishing the support of her strong titanium leg. "Nope. I think I can safely say that Conrad is gone for good. Even a little too good, in my opinion." She grinned and followed Professor Tooth down the front stairs.

A warm May sun was setting into the Pacific when Darrell and her friends decided on a final walk on the beach. They wound their way down the twisting path to the shore, Delaney thundering ahead in the lead.

"What a day," said Brodie, taking a deep breath of salt air.

"What a year," said Kate. She nudged Darrell, who was trailing slightly behind the others. "There's so much I just don't understand yet. Why were the Jewish people persecuted during the Inquisition?"

"Jewish people have been persecuted for centuries," said Darrell. "The Inquisition everywhere in Europe was a terrible thing. The only good thing was that because of it, changes took place. People like Martin Luther rose up against the wrongs that the church perpetuated, and elsewhere the common people ended up fighting the rule of absolute monarchs." She sighed. "I wish I knew the whole story. I feel so sick about Anne. She'd only been married three years and she was mother to one of the greatest queens England ever had. And when Henry got tired of her, he had her head chopped off just because it suited him."

"I read that when they buried her the box was too small so they had to tuck her head in beside the body," said Kate. "That man must have been a monster."

"I don't think he really was a monster," said Darrell. "He was a man brought up to believe that he was answerable to no one but God — and even then he fought to become leader of the church in England. His word was the law."

"I think he was a monster," said Kate firmly. "He divorced or killed five wives and died on the sixth, and all to satisfy his need for a son to rule after he was gone." She raised an eyebrow. "From what I've read, his daughter Elizabeth did as good a job as any man."

"And she had red hair," teased Paris.

"He changed religion in England forever," said Darrell. "Monster or not — the world is not the same place it was before he was in it." She kicked a pebble along the sand. "I'd also like to know what happened to Lady Jacqueline. Did she escape through Traitor's Gate and make it back to her family?"

"There's so much we'll never know," said Kate with a sigh. "You were there the most, Darrell. Do you think the Catholic Church was doing the right thing?"

"They thought so."

"And what about the Moors? The Christians wanted to fight the Moors because they were Muslim, right?"

Darrell nodded. "That was a large part of it. It's weird, you know. We got a chance to go back and see these massive changes right as they were taking place. The Inquisition changed the world forever, and the Protestant Reformation did too. But for all the torture and pain and loss — I feel like we haven't really learned our lesson, y'know?"

"No — I don't know," argued Paris. "I thought travelling through time was amazing. It was about fun — not about learning lessons."

Darrell laughed. "I meant we as a people — the human race. All the agony that went into changing the church and the way people are ruled, and five hundred years later my mom is still having to work for an organization that goes to wartorn countries to help promote peace. We never seem to know the whole story."

Kate stopped and put her hand against one of the giant boulders, sun baked and warm. "What is the whole story?" she whispered.

Brodie leaned against the boulder and smiled. "Darrell's right. It was all those things — and more. But how many people do you know that got to see a part of it for themselves?"

He turned to Darrell. "How was your mom's trip? Is she coming to get you tomorrow?"

Darrell nodded and gave a little sigh. "She's great — better than great, she tells me. I guess while I was facing off with the Duke of Norfolk, she was having a crisis of her own. A bomb went off in a bus outside her hospital. Oh, she was okay," Darrell said quickly, seeing her friends' horrified faces. "David was there to help her get back into the hospital, and she ended up saving a number of the casualties."

Darrell reached down and stroked Delaney's warm fur.

"I get the feeling she's going to marry the guy," she said quietly. "And I guess that's okay. He's been pretty good at helping her stay safe, and maybe she needs somebody more than just me to look after, too."

"Well," said Paris, turning his face to the setting sun and stretching like a cat, "I for one have had enough of living in the past for now. I'm ready to spend some time water-skiing this summer."

As Kate and Brodie weighed in on the relative merits of assorted water sports, Darrell and Delaney walked to the narrow mouth of the cave. *I've had enough of living in the past, too,* she thought. *My own past, anyway.*

She felt the thump of Delaney's gently waving tail as she looked up the cliff, past the old arbutus to where the windows of Eagle Glen shone with an impossible brilliance in the setting sun.

"Besides, Delaney-boy," she said, her hand brushing the thick ruff of his fur, "I think there might be a little exploring still to do around Eagle Glen, don't you?"